Barry Cornwall, Coventry Patmore

Bryan Waller Procter

An Autobiographical Fragment and Biographical Notes

Barry Cornwall, Coventry Patmore

Bryan Waller Procter
An Autobiographical Fragment and Biographical Notes

ISBN/EAN: 9783744688208

Printed in Europe, USA, Canada, Australia, Japan

Cover: Foto ©Raphael Reischuk / pixelio.de

More available books at **www.hansebooks.com**

BRYAN WALLER PROCTER

(BARRY CORNWALL).

AN

AUTOBIOGRAPHICAL FRAGMENT

AND

BIOGRAPHICAL NOTES,

WITH

PERSONAL SKETCHES OF CONTEMPORARIES, UNPUB-
LISHED LYRICS, AND LETTERS OF
LITERARY FRIENDS.

BOSTON:
ROBERTS BROTHERS.
1877.

EDITOR'S PREFACE.

I HAVE been asked — and the request, from the circumstances, has the force of a command — to edit the following memoranda by Mr. Procter relating to himself and his contemporaries, and to accompany them by a few remarks, biographical and otherwise, of my own. My only qualification for this task lies in the fact of my having known and loved Mr. Procter for more than thirty years. Inasmuch as he was, during that period, the friend of almost every person of character in art or letters, and as I saw less of him, owing to my having lived nearly always out of London, than many of his friends did, this qualification seems to me to be an inadequate one. But of that I have not been allowed to judge. For this reason, and because I have

been obliged to work in the country and
without means of verifying dates, etc., I claim
the forbearance of criticism in regard to the
defects in my execution of this dear and
honorable task.

C. P.

February 1, 1877.

CONTENTS.

———◆———

PART I.

viii CONTENTS.

CHAPTER IV.

(continued).

PART II.

RECOLLECTIONS OF LITERARY MEN.

PART III.

UNPUBLISHED VERSES.

PART IV.

LETTERS FROM LITERARY FRIENDS.

FROM A POEM

ADDRESSED TO "BARRY CORNWALL" BY W. S. LANDOR.

BARRY! your spirit long ago
Has haunted me; at last I know
The heart it springs from : one more sound
Ne'er rested on poetic ground.
But Barry Cornwall! by what right
Wring you my heart and dim my sight,
And make me wish at every touch
My poor old hand could do as much?
No other in these later times
Has bound me in so potent rhymes.
I have observed the curious dress
And jewelry of brave Queen Bess,
But always found some o'ercharged thing,
Some flaw in even the richest ring.
Admiring in her men of war
A rich but too argute guitar.
Our foremost now are more prolix,
And scrape with three-ell fiddlesticks,
And whether bound for griefs or smiles,
Are slow to turn as crocodiles.
Once every court and country bevy
Chose their gallants of loins less heavy,

And would have laid upon the shelf
Him who could talk but of himself.
Reason is stout; but even Reason
May walk too long in Rhymes' hot season:
I have heard many folks aver
They have caught horrid colds with her.
Imagination's paper kite,
Unless the string is held in tight,
Whatever fits and starts it takes,
Soon bounces on the ground and breaks.
You, placed afar from each extreme,
Nor dully drowse, nor idly dream,
But, ever flowing with good humor,
Are bright as Spring and warm as Summer.
Mid your Penates, not a word
Of scorn or ill report is heard,
Nor is there any need to pull
A sheaf or grass from cart too full.

*   *   *   *   *

W. S. Landor.

LETTER AND VERSES

By Mr. Algernon C. Swinburne.

MY DEAR SIR, — I send you some verses written a day
since on reading Charles Lamb's sonnet to you, and remem-
bering what you said (in jest) to Mr. Bayard Taylor and
myself the other day about your poetry being now less well
known than it had been, my tribute is less worth having, but
not less sincere ; so perhaps you will take it and excuse it as
what it is, an impromptu.

Yours very truly,

ALGERNON C. SWINBURNE.

To B. W. Procter (Barry Cornwall),
  September 1, 1868.

In vain men tell us time can alter
Old loves, or make old memories falter,
  That with the old year the old year's life closes.
The old dew still falls on the old sweet flowers,
The old sun revives the new-fledged hours,
  The old summer rears the new-born roses.

Much more a muse that bears upon her
Raiment and wreath and flower of honor,
  Gathered long since and long since woven,

Fades not or falls as falls the vernal
Blossoms that bear no fruit eternal,
　　By summer or winter charred or cloven.

No time casts down, no time upraises,
Such loves, such memories, and such praises
　　As need no grace of sun or shower,
No saving screen from frost or thunder,
To tend and house around and under
　　The imperishable and peerless flower.

Old thanks, old thoughts, old aspirations
Outlive men's lives, and lives of nations,
　　Dead, but for one thing which survives —
The inalienable and unpriced treasure,
The old joy of power, the old pride of pleasure,
　　That lives in light above men's lives.

A. C. SWINBURNE.

PART I.

---•---

AUTOBIOGRAPHICAL FRAGMENTS

BIOGRAPHICAL NOTES.

1

BRYAN WALLER PROCTER.

PART I.

AUTOBIOGRAPHICAL FRAGMENTS AND BIOGRAPHICAL NOTES.

A MAN may earn the gratitude of the world by speaking, writing, or acting admirably, but its most delighted and enduring thanks are given to individuality of character; in other words, to a living addition to the visible scope and variety of humanity. This individuality, whether in action or in art, is always more or less, and is often wholly, unconscious. Consciousness is the destruction of individuality, and converts it into its mockery, mannerism or oddity, which is not attached by any living fibre to that common nature in which true individuality has a tap-root of unknown depth. Individuality of character, or, in short, character, — since all true character

is individual, and incapable of being acquired by
any amount of effort, or quite abolished by any
amount of neglect, — is so rare and delicate a
quality that to be able to recognize it at first hand
in a poem or other work of art is in itself a sort
of originality, the gift, or rather the grace, of the
few whose verdict is sure to prevail after a time,
commonly a long time. Immediate and popular
admiration, indeed, is in most cases based upon a
semblance of individuality, and the greatest immediate reputations are therefore the result of the
combination of brilliant talent with some peculi-
arity of manner which seems to stamp it as genius.
It is different with *personal* individuality, which
is nothing other than genius in life and action.
When this is at all strongly pronounced, as it was
in Charles Lamb and his friend Procter, its manifestation appears at so many points, and affects
others so constantly and peremptorily, even when it
is most unassuming, that *not* to recognize it would
imply a rare degree of insensibility. When, as
in Lamb and Procter, the individuality is common
to private character and published work, then
fame and popularity start hand in hand and almost at once ; for every acquaintance made by such
men becomes a thoroughly convinced apostle of

their genius and champion of their reputation.
It is true that in all men of genius or true individuality, the personal character is the fountain
of, and fundamentally identical with, the peculiar
character of their poetry, painting, etc.; but there
are many circumstances which may prevent its
development and display in their life and manners without withdrawing its halo from their
works. To this class of great men the world is
long in awarding their fame. Their ways cast
suspicion on their works; and the reputation of a
man of genius who lacks in his life the courage
or the habits of his inspirations may suffer for
generations, or even for ever, if his biography
happens to have been such and so written as to
go down to posterity with his truer self.

No one who has passed an hour in the company
of Charles Lamb's "dear boy" can ever lose the
impression made upon him by that simple, sincere,
shy, and delicate soul. His small figure, his head,
not remarkable for much besides its expression of
intelligent and warm good-will, and its singular
likeness to that of Sir Walter Scott; his conversation, which had little decision or "point" in the
ordinary sense, and often dwelt on truths which a
novelty-loving society banishes from its repertory

as truisms, never disturbed the effect, in any assemblage, of his real distinction. His silence seemed wiser, his simplicity subtler, his shyness more courageous than the wit, philosophy, and assurance of others. When such a man expressed himself more or less faithfully in a series of gracious poems, of which he alone, of all his circle, did not seem proud, it naturally followed that all who knew him were eager to declare and extend the credit and honor to which he had aspired with so much simplicity, and which he bore with so entire an absence of self-assertion. The tradition of such a character has the power of lingering in the world, even when the life has been so uneventful as to leave little scope for biography or even for anecdote. And the writings which are the outcome of that character are floated down by such tradition to a posterity which might never have heard of them but for this proof of their genuineness.

The "events" of Bryan Waller Procter's life might all be told in a very few pages — unless, indeed, his friendships may be regarded as its events.* Concerning some of these he wrote, in

* The following is a limited selection from the list of Mr. Procter's personal friends and acquaintance. Byron,

his old age, the " Recollections," which form the most significant part of this volume. He has also left a sketch of his own life from infancy to early manhood. But he was the last man in the world to write an autobiography. He says much more of his old tutor, M. Molière, than he says of himself, and exhibits, throughout the piece, a thoroughly characteristic indisposition to dwell for a moment on his own deeds, thoughts, and feelings. The reader will regret this the more, inasmuch as it seems impossible to supply from other sources the information in which this sketch is deficient. The contemporaries of his youth are

Wordsworth, Coleridge, Bowles, Keats, Crabbe, Rogers, Campbell, Hogg, Cary, Milman, Leigh Hunt, Hood, Southey, Landor, Sir Walter Scott, Talfourd, Beddoes, Hartley Coleridge, the first and second Lords Lytton, Allan Cunningham, R. H. Horne, Matthew Arnold, Tennyson, Browning, Swinburne, Gabriel Rossetti, Lord Houghton, Aubrey de Vere, Sir Thomas Lawrence, Stothard, Landseer, Turner, Cattermole, Eastlake, Haydon, Leighton, Millais, Holman Hunt, Hallam, Grote, Spedding, Macaulay, Carlyle, Lord Jeffrey, Edward Irving, Charles Lamb, George Dyer, Godwin, Hazlitt, Peacock, Kinglake, G. S. Venables, Julius Hare, D'Israeli the elder, Dr. Croly, Dickens, Thackeray, De Quincey, Henry Reeve, Fonblanque, Lockhart, Sydney Smith, James and Horace Smith, Galt, Mendelssohn, Moscheles, Benedict, John Kemble, Liston, Charles Kemble, Macready, Storey.

all dead, and he was as reticent, concerning himself, towards his friends as he was towards the public, for whom it is to be presumed that he intended the following chapters: —

.

AUTOBIOGRAPHICAL SKETCH.

"CHAPTER I.

" My progenitors resided for many years in one of the northern counties, Yorkshire or Cumberland. I do not know of any ancestors whom I have any right to boast of; they were small farmers during many generations. I have sometimes, I confess, wished that I could trace my origin to some loftier source — a great poet, or historian, or artist; to some Sir Philip Sidney, who gave water to the soldier of Zutphen, or to some Columbus, who discovered a world. But I have no such hope. There was, indeed, one youth, — no lineal ancestor, however, but some collateral relation, — who exhibited signs or promise of being a sculptor, but he died before he achieved any settled fame; so I was left to carve out a·

reputation for myself, although I had small material and little ambition to do so.

"I might, I believe, trace my blood (partly) through one channel of undoubted gentry, but this source was one I do not care to boast of, scarcely to refer to. My father was one of several children; the best amongst the males, as I have reason to think. He had moderate abilities and somewhat scanty education, having been taught only writing and arithmetic, and a little Latin. I knew this, although he died many years ago, from the circumstance of his examining me occasionally in figures, and in my early Latin books. There being, I imagine, small prospect of his rising to any ambitious height in the country, he threw his fortune upon a hazard, and came up straight to London. There he at first entered a merchant's counting-house; then he ventured, for a short period, on some species of merchandise. In that region of loss and gain he remained only a very short time, until some bequest, or other accident of luck, came and enabled him to subside into a private station, where he lived unoccupied and independent for many years. He had only to receive his rents and dividends, and to overlook the growing up of his children. Of these there were three — myself, a sister (who is dead), and a younger brother, who afterwards succeeded to the possession of a small landed estate, and who all his life has been an idle man.

" One word more, however, before I part with my parents altogether. My father, although not a man of remarkable ability, possessed the most uncompromising honesty I ever met with. He was not generous, perhaps, but he was true; earnest and true. In word, or deed, or thought he never, in my belief, deviated from the strict truth, the simple fact. He could not, I sincerely think, say or do anything that was untrue or dishonest.

" My mother was simply the kindest and tenderest mother in the world.

" I am entitled, however, to speak only of myself. Let me be brief. Nothing particularly marked my childhood. I was found to be much as boys usually are. Nothing distinguished from others of the same age. It seemed my destiny to float along from the cradle to the grave on the happy stream of mediocrity. My tastes, even as I recollect, were common enough. My senses were indeed attracted by the scent of the violet, the April grass and flowers ; I heard music in the winds, and running river; otherwise I marched quietly onwards in the great crowds of human life, with my undiscovered destiny before me. I had few friends and no flatterers; no father or aunt ever deluded my imagination that the seeds of genius were lurking within me. Such I was, when very young (almost too young), sent to a small boarding-school near London. This was at A——, and it contained thirty boys of various ages, ranging from seven to fifteen, or more. I myself was scarcely more than five years old. Of course, I knew nothing beyond my letters, or a little easy reading, which I had acquired mainly from a Bible full of pictures.

" In this school there presided an old master, whose duties were limited almost exclusively to matters of finance. He was, in fact, the proprietor of the establishment, and managed its expenditure and general economy. Three undermasters or ushers taught and controlled the boys in the school. I have the most accurate recollection of each. Matters of infinitely greater importance have long since faded away and been forgotten, but the pictures and characters of these men, after the lapse of seventy years, remain vivid and clear. Mr. H——, who taught Latin, from the grammar to the Æneid, had taken his degree at Oxford. He was about twenty-seven years of age, and was pale and sickly. I think he was consumptive ; there seemed scarcely space sufficient between his breast and his shoulders to enable him to cough freely. This cough, however, was very frequent, and in order to allay it, he was obliged to resort to a large phial of medicine (which he kept in his desk) whenever it was troublesome. He had a kind nature, a gentle and very sad look. His eyes, which were originally gray, were lustreless and faded ; the orbs were apparently without lymph.

" M——, who taught English, writing, and arithmetic, had been, at an earlier period of his life, a lieutenant in the Navy. He had a deep jaw, a severe countenance, a temper never gentle, and at all times easily overset. He was fond of stimulants, and had the most undisguised contempt for the small beer of the establishment.

" And now I come to dear old Monsieur Molière, who was our instructor in French. Never let me forget him, his patience, or his kindness. He was about fifty years of age, had a somewhat dark complexion, a Roman nose, and a gentle and very expressive mouth, which looked as if it were (as indeed it was) the property of a gentleman. I never, heard a cross or vulgar word from his mouth; never saw an impatient look in his face. He was scarcely accessible to a joke; indeed, the only instance in which he ever exhibited any appearance of humor was when he offered his large snuff-box to one of the young boys, and smiled at the effects of the titillating grains on the tender and unpractised muscles.

" Monsieur Molière was a French emigrant. I do not know much of his former history, but I believe he belonged to the middle class of society. . . . . The Goddess Fortune had never spoiled him. She left him the ability to labor and endure; perhaps these were nearly all his poor possessions.

" The schoolmaster is generally a compound of the martyr and the tyrant. . . . . Monsieur M—— was not one of this general class, however. He was accustomed to interest himself in the games as well as the lessons of the boys. He sympathized with all our pleasures, whilst he mollified our pains. It was, indeed, necessary that he should occupy himself with other things besides his own recollections, for these were melancholy enough; for when no school duty engaged him, and he walked up and down the capacious playground, the

curious bystander could sometimes espy tears in
his serious gray eyes — meditative drops.   At
those times we imagined that his mind sank
inwards — went back, far away, into former happy
years — resting, perhaps, on a wife or child, lost or
dead ; sacrificed possibly to that bloody Moloch,
who was then worshipped throughout France.

" Molière was naturally, I think, of a cheerful
turn of mind.   At all events, an apparent cheerfulness lighted up his countenance occasionally.
And he had one or two small pleasures.   He was
fond of flowers, — mignonette or myrtle, — and
when the warmer season allowed of these being
purchased cheaply, we saw him often wear a small
sprig of these in the breast of his coat; and these
he would introduce proudly to some of the elder
boys who pretended to appreciate flowers.

" I scarcely know why I recall these things,
which have been undisturbed in my recollection
for more than half a century.   Suddenly, however,
there rises up out of the oblivious mist of time the
figure of the kind, uncomplaining old man. . . . .
I see him with his large side curls, and his fawn-
colored coat, always neat, yet always threadbare,
which the smallness of his salary did not wholly
account for.   It was surmised by some of us that

he divided his earnings with some of his countrymen, poorer even than himself, whom the tyranny
of the times had driven to England. This,
however, was known only to his own heart, for
he had no confidant in his charities.

"We never saw money in his possession, beyond one or two very small silver coins. These
he kept in a large old silk purse, which was
displayed only when some case of extreme distress
urged him to expend a bounteous sixpence. After
these gifts (when in summer) we fancied that we
never saw the customary sprig of myrtle. There
was only the old threadbare, fawn-colored coat
wrapped round his warm and tender heart.

"I wish that I had more ample materials to enable me to become his historian. But I have not.
Let these, therefore, be taken for his little epitaph.
I must here dismiss my poor old French master,
for I cannot pause to acknowledge all the benefits
which I and others derived from him. These
were not of the ordinary kind, such as a poor
scholar extracts from his teacher. The good
which is effused by a kind nature is not lost or
wasted in vacancy. The surrounding natures
must catch a portion of it, as of a portion of the
sun or air, and diffuse it in their turn.

" When poor Molière and H—— left the school, our number of ushers was diminished, and a Monsieur D—— undertook to cane the boys into Latin and French also. He was a tall, coarse-faced fellow (French or Swiss), upwards of six feet in height, and had a strong resemblance to a bandit. I saw little of him, for he had scarcely begun to be fully detested when I left the little school at A——. It was about that time that the school itself began to decline, and it finally (shortly afterwards) became extinct.

" CHAPTER II.

" WHEN I was about thirteen years of age I awoke and found myself in a larger institution, a public school.* It was very large, and comprehended a great variety of boys. Apart from their mere moral and physical distinctions, which of course were numerous, they came to us from all places and ranks in life. Some from ancient heights (lordly, even ducal); some from agricultural eminences — county families or humbler gentry;

* Harrow.

and a few were of the plebeian order from the plain. These last, nevertheless, were quite capable of maintaining their equality (for all boys are presumptively on a level) with those who were socially above them.

" In this school, with no very promising outlook, I remained fixed for about four years. I had no wealth in the vulgar sense, very few riches in the intellectual. Some activity of body, indeed, and a little mental curiosity, in common with others, were mine. But these did not carry me beyond my fellow boys, who were all racing towards the same goal.

" I confess that I had not any preternatural vision which enabled me to see into the depths or obscurities of things. . . . . The daily task, the daily meal, the regular hours of sleep and exercise or idleness were all sufficient in themselves for me. I had nothing of that feverish, unwholesome temperament which spurs the scholar into worlds beyond his reach, and which is sometimes called genius ; not much even of that vigorous ambition which tempts him into the accessible regions which are just above him ; yet I was not without daring.

" There were three long vacations, which few of

2   B

us had purchased by any great expense of labor. Mine were spent almost invariably at the house of my mother's uncle, who lived about a dozen miles from London. It was a spacious house, and had one or two very large apartments and an extensive garden, in which I used to recreate in all weathers. One of those apartments was a bedroom (the spare room), and was distinguished by an old-fashioned paper which suggested many wonderful thoughts; indeed, it was not without its terrors, for strange faces and objects, partaking at once of the bird and the beast, looked out of it, and somewhat disturbed my waking hours. I was occasionally left in this room as a sleeping region, under the idea that I should enjoy quiet rest. But it was not so. My imagination had begun to move. Some things which were beautiful, and many things which were terrible, operated very sensibly upon me. My brain was disturbed. I began to dream, and to recollect my dreams, and to dwell upon them, and strove to discover their meanings and origin.

" How vividly I still recollect the fields and gardens through which I used to ramble. How fresh were the meadows!

" In my uncle's family there was a female

servant, occupying no very high position, but
endowed with an acute intellect, far beyond her
station.   She was beyond all doubt superior in
intellect to the other inhabitants of the house.   If
her master and mistress had known her thoroughly,
they must have succumbed beneath the genius of
Alice W——.

" This woman was the daughter of a man who
had failed in a profession or business.   Having
had much leisure in early life, she had cultivated
her taste for reading.   She knew some of the
historians and poets, and all the productions of
Richardson and Fielding, and narrated their
stories fluently and emphatically, and with marvellous taste and discrimination of the characters.
But above all — high above all — she worshipped
Shakespeare.   She it was who first taught me to
know him and to love him, and led eventually to
my wondering admiration for the greatest genius
that the world has ever produced.   She used to
repeat to me whole scenes, selecting those best
adapted to a boy's apprehension.   In particular I
remember what effect was produced on me by her
recitation of passages in ' Hamlet,' and of the
scenes between Hubert and Arthur in ' King John.'

" ' I will buy a Shakespeare with the first money

that I get,' said I. 'And you cannot do better,'
replied she. This was not a mere threat, but a
resolution that was accomplished soon after. I
bought a Shakespeare, and entered into a world
beyond my own. I think I saw (I know that I
felt) many of his gentler beauties, the nice distinctions of character, not perhaps his sublimer
thoughts, not even his deeper passions. . . . .

"But I had not leisure to study or worship my
Shakespeare long, for at the end of a month or six
weeks my destiny drove me back to school.

"The ordinary holidays (of a day or half a day's
duration) were of course spent at or in the neighborhood of the school. Thus, with every Saint's
day also transmuted into a half-holiday, the periods
of study were brief enough; and when to this is
added the facts, that sometimes one master had to
superintend a whole class of boys, however large,
and that after breakfast the morning school-time
(the principal one) scarcely, if at all, exceeded
half an hour, the opportunities for examination of
each boy were quite insufficient. The fourth form,
in my time, consisted of from fifty to eighty
scholars, about six or seven of whom only were
'called up' and examined during school-time,
their lessons having been construed beforehand

to them by their private tutor. Sometimes a week (even a fortnight) has elapsed without a boy having been examined at all. The consequence of this was that many 'chanced it;' in less equivocal language, ran the risk of being forgotten, and expended their leisure out of 'school hours' in happy idleness.

" There was no incentive. As for any ambition to excel, it existed only in games, where successful competition was attended by immediate victory and by the applause of equals. . . . I will not shrink from boasting that when young I attained some excellence at football; that in leaping and running I was distinguished; and finally, that I was considered a formidable antagonist in the mild and modest game of marbles. But in these matters we were (mentally) as naked as the athlete; no poisoned dagger; no secret weapon; no fraud; no unwholesome stratagem.

" Our fights were behind the school. These never took place amongst the highest boys, who imagined themselves men, and contemplated in future times another mode of deciding their quarrels. Our fights, however, were sometimes stoutly contested amongst the lower (not always the younger) boys.

"The objects of learning in a public school are, I will not say utterly useless, but they occupy by far too great a portion of time for any useful purpose. With the exception of Greek and Latin, all languages are ignored, and all mathematical studies and history. They are totally excluded from school hours, which are solely occupied by Latin and Greek (dead languages), which absorb the time, and consequently force the minds of the boys from studies far more likely to expand and sharpen the general intellect.

"I must speak of the boys. It is not easy to characterize boys very minutely. They are known mostly by their appetites, by their wants and desires and dislikes, which rise up and show themselves every day, and are expressed in obvious language. I shall not particularize any by name, nevertheless I may state that there were two of them who became very remarkable. One * toiled and struggled upwards, till he became a Minister of State. Another † blossomed into a poet. There were, however, in the latter, during his school-time, no symptoms of such a destiny. He was loud, even coarse, and very capable of a boy's vulgar enjoyments. He played at hockey and

* Sir Robert Peel.   † Lord Byron.

racquets, and was occasionally engaged in pugilistic combats. . . . .

" For the most part, my schoolfellows were much alike; at all events they exhibited no very distinctive qualities. They drew from their homes generally the qualities which are reputed to belong to their class. To these (aristocratic or otherwise) were of course superadded those common virtues or vices which are luckily spread over the whole surface of man. Here, however, they appeared to show themselves in subjection to the class distinctions.

" Amongst the persons of whom I think it a duty, in a history of this sort, to paint an unbiassed portrait, I must not exclude myself. As far as I am able to compass such an heroic achievement, it shall be sincere. I was then neither very short nor very tall; neither handsome nor hideous. I had indeed when young some activity and a little courage; but all is gone.

" In reference to my intellect I may say, with my hand on my heart, I had nothing superfluous; nothing either very bad or very good; nothing very stupid or very bright. A little quickness once existed, as it does in most boys. But I never should have been a senior wrangler, nor a Smith's prizeman, nor had I any pretensions to trample on mediocre people. Then I was without ambition, — a fatal defect, and one which (as some critics say) argues a corresponding defect of intellect. If a man, they tell us, be capable of leaping or riding well, the chance is that he will have the desire of showing his riding or leaping. This is not an inevitable consequence, however. In meditating somewhat deeply on the subject, I find it difficult to distinguish myself from other boys of my own age. I never, I believe, had much covetousness, or envy; nor was I addicted to mean or (unusually) selfish thoughts. Assuredly I always disliked undue pretence and sordid tuft-hunting, and was — as I have already stated — without an atom of ambition. Even my small attempts at literature subsequently were unattended by ambitious thoughts. I always wrote from the mere pleasure of writing. I had no other stimulus.

"CHAPTER III.

" WHEN I left school, a long debate ensued as to whether I should proceed to college for a degree, or be sent into the country for a few years. A friend of my father (who was cursed with an extravagant son) advised the latter course. '*I* never learned much at Oxford,' said he, 'and my boy has learned nothing, — nothing except extravagant habits.' This determined my father, who had a very saving soul; and he thereupon made arrangements for my being sent into Wiltshire, and placed under the care of a professional man, a solicitor. The transition from the neighborhood of London to a country village is not at first thoroughly understood. After having dwelt at the distance of a few miles from the great city, we are removed, in the scarcely perceptible interval of a night's travel, to a new land. We pass through unadorned roads, through wastes or forests, to almost unpeopled places, where the rare occurrence of a few cottages offers no requital for the barren silence that dwells around. It is only after a little meditation that the pastures develop their various beauties, and the corn offers its golden stores to your notice. If it be early summer, you cannot long withstand the fragrance of the sheets of May, which spread out their white riches on every hawthorn. Nature, endlessly prolific Nature, assumes a new shape at every turn.

The violet in the first grass, the daisy in the meadow, the rose and honeysuckle blossom which enrich every hedge, feed your mind gradually with grace and sweetness and strength, until all your town armor of ignorance is cast aside. Your thoughts, which have hitherto been obscured by boyish things, become refined; your sight opens and admits wider sights and more gentle objects; your affection adopts the softer virtues; the body yields to the intellect; you rise from the dust at once.

"Richter it is, I think, who says that he never forgot the time when he first began to think. I imagine that I now arrived at this time. A thousand things which once came, and disappeared, and left no trace, now stamped their pictures on my mind. I now saw and pondered on the difficulties of things, and the wonders of the world, which suggested fancies and thoughts, and drove me into reasonings on things that formerly seemed to have no meaning. Let no one despise any means by which the intellect of a boy may be widened or strengthened. We attach too exclusive a value to words and figures. The mathematics are very valuable, and the Greek and Latin languages deserve some study (not too much); but what teacher has ever endeavored to instil into his pupils the value of weeds or grasses, of animal or vegetable nature; . . . the wonders of space, or of the seasons; of night, of silence? All the histories usually taught in schools are of nations or bodies of men (which seldom or never interest the reader); not of individual suffering or heroism, which alone can stir the heart to its depths, and compel it by sympathy to remember. We love or pity individuals (not multitudes), and we cannot, if we would, forget them.

" The gentleman in whose house I resided in Wiltshire was a man of real but unobtrusive intellect; and his manners were plain and unaffected. I am ashamed to say that at first I thought him a somewhat vulgar man. I was utterly mistaken. Indeed, it was not long before I discovered that he had qualities which were superior to my own. If he had less of ornament, he had quite as much intellect and as much delicacy as I had. Then he was kind and irresistibly honest. I began to hope that I might acquire these virtues. . . .

" Not many events occurred in the country that enable me to mark the progress of my mind; but some caused a deep impression on me. Once I saw a child sicken and die, and I had to convey it to a supposed healthy place, and afterwards to bring its little body to its mother's home. At another time I witnessed a dreadful surgical operation. It was an amputation. By the aid of these and other distresses, I began to learn something of the nature of compassion. The people of the village were not distinguished by any remarkable qualities; assuredly not by any great ones. They ran the race of life — steadily, quietly — in the general mêlée. I do not remember a scholar — scarcely a dunce. No one was an expert, even in crime.

" The profession for which I was destined was the law. It deals with rights and wrongs and with forms and precedents. It may refer to prosperity or misfortune, but does not deal intimately with the affections. In earthly justice there is no pity. It is defective in nice distinctions. The gradations in crimes are not minute enough to satisfy tender morality; and there are some faults which are not crimes at all. If a father kills a son, or a son kills his father, it is punished simply as a common murder. If the wealthy father banishes the son and allows him to die from want, no special punishment is awarded; nothing but the contempt of the world. So if he settles his large estate on his eldest son and bequeaths his daughter to the parish, there is the same immunity.

" In some cases general contempt takes the place of punishment, but there is no obligation on a man to do good, nor to abstain from doing evil. These questions lie between him and God.

" Beyond a certain point all is *terra incognita.* The judgment of a youth becomes perplexed. The many things which have been expounded to him, as good and evil, distract his imagination. What could I determine in these cases, but read the volumes which charmed me, abandon earthly legal doubts and dull uninteresting facts for the region of fiction? And now I must confess that my ideas of life, of right or wrong, received the greatest help from a source seemingly insignificant. I had before in my early youth read the greater part of the greatest poet in the world, Shakespeare; all his tragedies, for his comedies suit a maturer age. The terrible and other passions, however, at that time, exceeded my young sympathy, which at first is always imperfect. As the intellect acquires its size and strength only with age — so it is with the affections and the passions. The heart of a man is wider than that of a child.

In the village where I dwelt there was a circulating library. Its contents were of a very humble description. It contained the novels and romances of fifty years ago, a score of old histories, and a few volumes of biography now forgotten. The books had been bought at sales for the value of waste paper. Nevertheless, it was out of this dusty collection of learning that I was enabled to select a few books which spurred me on the great road of thought. When we encounter a new idea it surprises us, and we begin to doubt and examine it — and this is thought. For it is not simply the admission of another man's ideas, for these sometimes present themselves so that we neither dissent nor sympathize. They do not spur the mind on its road at all.

"I had already read Cæsar and Virgil and Ovid, and some parts of Theocritus, and passages of Homer; but these passed unprofitable over my mind, like shadows over the unreflecting earth below. They were read as words only, and left no trace or image. But now a more effective agent was at work, which moved my heart at the same time with my other faculties. Let no one despise the benefits which thus open the young and tender heart. They are the gates of knowledge. . . .

If I had never become intimate with Le Sage and
Fielding and Richardson, with Sterne and Inchbald and Radcliffe, I should perhaps have stopped
at my seventeenth year disheartened on my way.
But they were my encouragers; they forced me to
travel onwards to the Intellectual Mountains. I
have now forgotten all my mathematics and
arithmetic, all my Greek, and almost all my
Latin; but I cleave to those who were true
nurses of my boyhood still.

"CHAPTER IV.

" THE profession for which I was intended was
the law, but I regret to say that, with certain little
intervals of study, my time was absorbed by
amusing books. I read all the English poets, from
Chaucer down to Burns. Almost all the classics
which had been converted into English ; most of
the histories accessible to English readers ; and all
the novels and romances then extant, without a
single exception. From such a groundwork my
future might have been easily anticipated. Accordingly I threw myself into letters. I began with
verse. . . . I did not succeed eminently, yet I did

not altogether fail. Of course I dwelt on the tor-
tures of the affections, and eventually dwelt on
love. To enable me to speak authentically on this
subject, it was necessary to enter one of the Dan-
tesque circles of Hades which are so full of torment.

" As a step in philosophy, and in order to render
myself thoroughly acquainted with trouble, I fell
in love. This pleasant pain, of which all poets
have spoken, was mine. I am ashamed to say
how temporary it was. But what can one do at
eighteen ? I would have suffered longer if I could.
But it was not to be. Destiny and the nature of
youth were against me. There is no authentic
history that I remember in which the pains of
love, or vanity, in very young men (boys rather)
have endured long or terminated fatally. In this
respect the old classic histories fail. Even Hylas
and Narcissus were too young to die. Well,
falling in love about the 1st of April, it was as a
matter of course that the festival of St. Valentine
should not pass unrecorded. I wish that I had preserved this ' first fault ' as it was called at school.

" When I was about nineteen or twenty I came
to London to live. I will not detain the reader
with my numerous doubts and changes of opinion
(which I called speculations), but advance at

once to the period when I settled down and thought of literature as a profession. A serious illness had distracted me for some time from my legal studies, but my meditations on literary men and literary projects were uninterrupted. I began to think. About this time I made the acquaintance of two or three writers whose dinners were furnished by their pens. At first I looked with humble veneration on these imaginary geniuses, whose goose-quills served them so effectually in life. I coveted their acquaintance and friendship. One of these gentlemen, an Irishman, was a most violent combatant with his pen. Another was editor of a monthly magazine. A third was a busy idler in letters; not a laborer. Amongst these three men, toiling in the same field with myself, I could not after a most careful examination discover much to admire. They had some envy, and a vast deal of prejudice, and a handsome crop of faults. Facility they had acquired by long practice, but little more. Words came to them at will. My humility began to disappear. Intimacy corrected my first scrutiny. . . . I perceived that the mysteries which encircle literature were not as formidable as those which surrounded the temple of Eleusis. . . . The longer we look at

2* c

the criticisms on books, the ignorance or injustice
on the one hand and the flagrant partiality on the
other, the more we are perplexed. Do you imagine, O youth, that your merit will bring down the
ivy wreath of praise upon you? Do you imagine
that knowledge of your subject will deter adverse
decision? Collect yourself, my friend; know that
the roads to fortune are always uncertain. The
world is not gazing at you with all its eyes. It
has other things to contemplate."

Here the autobiographical sketch comes to an
end.

From the time when Mr. Procter "came to
London to live" (that is, about 1807) to 1815,
when he began to contribute the poems, which
first brought him into public notice, to the "Literary Gazette," no record remains of his course of
life, beyond the very vague and scanty indications
in the last paragraph of the foregoing fragment,
from which it is to be inferred that his law studies
during much of that time were held more or less
completely in abeyance by his experiments in literature. There are, however, one or two points
upon which it is possible to supplement this
meagre account of the poet's youth.

His little essay on " The Death of Friends " contains passages which are evidently autobiographical: " I remember, when I was about four years of age, how I learned to spell, and was sent daily in the servant's hand to a little day school. . . . I had no ambition then, no hatred, no uncharitableness. . . . I had no *organs* for such things ; yet now I can hate almost as strongly as I love, and am as constant to my antipathies as to my affections."

This is an almost amusingly characteristic sentence. Mr. Procter liked to be thought " a good hater," simply because it really was not one of his strong points. He was an ideal hater, but a very practical lover of his fellows ; and the somewhat artificial emphasis of this " virtue " in some of his songs shows it to have savored slightly of hypocrisy. He was the last man to make a boast or demonstration of the virtues he really possessed. He goes on to say :

" When my fifth was running into my sixth year, and I was busied with parables and scripture history (the only food which nourished my infant mind), I was much noticed by a young person, a female. I was at that time living with an old relation in H——shire, and I still preserve the recollection of Miss R——'s tender condescension towards me. She was a pretty, delicate girl, and very amiable ; and I became — yes, it is true, for I remember the strong feelings of that time — *enamoured* of her. My love had the fire of passion, but not the clay which drags it downwards ; it partook of the innocence of my years, while it etherealized me. Whether it was the divinity of beauty that stung me, or rather that lifted me above the darkness and immaturity of childhood, I know not; but my feelings were anything but childish. By some strong intuition I felt that there was a difference (I knew not what) that called forth an extraordinary and impetuous regard."

These infantine passions, almost peculiar to and perhaps almost invariably occurring in the childhood of poets, are events of extreme importance in the history of their souls ; and the world is probably indebted for one of its very highest blessings, namely, the imaginative glory which irradiates its idea of love, to the fact that the poets, who are mainly the originators and promulgators of that idea, have had this singular capacity for loving, with the full vehemence of passion, in the innocence and ignorance of early childhood ;

their manhood retaining, amid all its error and obscuration, the happy memory of that smokeless flame. In the present instance, death joined with love in lifting the soul of the infant poet into that sweet and pure atmosphere from which it never afterwards descended. He thus pursues his story:

"The last time I ever saw her was (as well as I can recollect) in October, or late in September. I was told that Miss R—— was ill, was *very* ill, and that perhaps I might not see her again. Death I could not, of course, comprehend; but I understood perfectly what was a perpetual absence from my pretty friend. Whether I wept or raved, or how it was, I know not; but I was taken to visit her. It was a cold day, and the red and brown leaves were plentiful on the trees, and it was afternoon when we arrived at an old-fashioned country-house (something better than a farm-house), which stood at some distance from the high road. The sun was near his setting; but the whole of the wide west was illuminated, and threw crimson and scarlet colors on the windows, over which hung a cloud of vine-stalks and changing leaves that dropped by scores on every summons of the blast. . . . She was sitting (as I entered) in a large arm-chair covered with white, like a faded Flora, and was looking at the sun; but she turned her bright and gentle looks on me, and the pink bloom dimpled on her cheek as she smiled and bade me welcome."

Miss R—— soon afterwards died. The narrator of this incident says nothing of the dumb depth of childish sorrow which must have followed. He never seemed able to fix his thoughts upon himself.

The poet's mother, who lived till 1837, used to relate that, in his earliest childhood — when only about four years old — his fondness for books was such that he would prefer them to his food, being with difficulty persuaded to leave the one for the other. What books they were is not now known. It is to be presumed — and hoped — that they were picture-books.

The first school he went to was a dame's school at Finchley, where he was living with his relatives. The place made so deep an impression on his affections, that when he was eighty he used to be taken out of London, and had himself drawn about in a chair there, in the vain hope of finding the house he had lived at, and the school of his infancy.

Most of Mr. Procter's intimate friends must have heard him refer, with more pride perhaps than he ever expressed in his other achievements, to the fact that, upon just occasion, he could. and did hold his own at Harrow by his pugilistic abilities; a circumstance to which he, no doubt, looked back with the greater satisfaction of conscience, inasmuch as he was somewhat undersized (though well-made), and highly sensitive in nerves. Witness the following anecdote. " He used," writes Miss Martineau, " to tell of the horrors which grew upon him, when he was twelve years old, as he became more and more persuaded that a raven in his father's garden haunted him, and played the spy upon him." The boy on one occasion felled the raven with some missile, and thought he had killed it; but was much relieved, soon afterwards, by seeing the bird of ill-omen strutting about and croaking as cheerlessly as if nothing had happened.

The " statesman " and the " poet " spoken of in the foregoing sketch as having been among his schoolfellows at Harrow, were Sir Robert Peel and Lord Byron. He used to relate how Peel undertook, on one occasion, to write for him an imposition of Latin verse for a consideration of half-a-crown; but whether the future great financier ever got paid was more than Mr. Procter could undertake to remember.

With Lord Byron, for whom, as a boy, he evidently had not much liking or admiration, he renewed his acquaintance in after years.

A valentine addressed to a young lady who lived next door to him at Calne seems to have been the first verse from which the young poet reaped a harvest of praise; and this he did under circumstances which gave him acute pleasure, for he managed unseen, to see it delivered, and to hear the shrieks of delight which accompanied its reading.

The name of the solicitor at Calne to whom the boy was articled was Atherton. This gentleman, on going once to the quarter-sessions, gave him a bag of papers to carry. This the youth declined to do, though he had evidently, from the foregoing little history, a great respect and affection for his employer. Mr. Atherton, without a word, proceeded to carry the bag himself, whereupon the pupil, in " a remorse of love," immediately seized upon it, and bore it cheerfully the rest of the way.

The poet's father died in the beginning of the year 1816. By this event the young man came into some property, and seems to have lived handsomely upon it. About this time he was again reading with a conveyancer, and was very soon

afterwards in partnership with a solicitor, a Mr.
Slaney. He took a house in Brunswick Square,
entertained his friends hospitably, kept a hunter,
and used to stay at St. Alban's in the hunting
season, improved his early excellence as a boxer by
taking lessons from a famous pugilist, Cribb,
passed much of his time with a family in Hertfordshire, and fell in love with one of the daughters,
to whom he dedicated the " Sicilian Story " in
1820, at which date, however, as it appears from
the verses themselves, this passion had subsided
into friendship.

> It may be that the rhymes I bring to thee
> (An idle offering, Beauty), are my last:
> Therefore, albeit thine eye may never cast
> Its light on them, 'tis fit thine image be
> Allied unto my song; for silently
> Thou may'st connect the present with the past.
> 'Tis fit, for Saturn now is hurrying fast,
> And thou may'st soon be nothing, e'en to me.
> Be this the record then of pleasant hours
> Departed, when beside the river shaded
> I walk'd with thee, gazing my heart away,
> And, from the sweetest of your garden flowers,
> Stole only those which on your bosom faded.
> O, why has happiness so short a day!

The poet's love for this lady seems not to have
reached beyond the imaginative phase; for no

offer of marriage was ever made by him to her.
In 1820 his partnership with the solicitor had
been dissolved, and he is said to have been
"living by his pen," and to have found it a very
irksome mode of life; but this seems only to
have been a temporary necessity, caused by losses
incurred through this partnership.   In 1824, when
he married, he had an income, arising from houses
left to him by his father, of about five hundred
a year.

As is not uncommon with men who are destined
to reach a great age, Procter, in his early manhood, was almost always in a weak or suffering
state of health.

"Barry Cornwall's" active career as a poet
may be said to have commenced with his connection with the "Literary Gazette," in 1815, and to
have ended with the publication of the "Flood of
Thessaly and other Poems," in 1823.   For though
his most enduring work, the "English Songs,"
first appeared in 1832, and many short pieces
were from time to time added to that collection,
the contents of this volume were the result of only
occasional effort during all the preceding years.
The "Dramatic Scenes," "Marcian Colonna,"
the "Sicilian Story," "Mirandola, a Tragedy,"

and the "Flood of Thessaly," all appeared between the years 1819 and 1823. It is not surprising that fame was swift in following so remarkable a display of facility in a high order of composition. The poet's crowning triumph was the production of his tragedy on the stage of Covent Garden Theatre. It was the event of the dramatic season. Macready played "Mirandola," Charles Kemble "Guido," Miss Foote "Isidora." The success on the first night was complete, and the play was acted sixteen times, which was a very good "run" in those days, when the theatre was mainly supported by wealthy and cultivated persons, who often went night after night to one or other of the two great houses, and would have ill-brooked the presentation of the same piece for a hundred consecutive evenings. The following is the poet's own account of this event:

"In the year 1821 I was silly enough to write a play. It was called "Mirandola," and was a very hurried and imperfect production. Had I taken pains, I could have made a much more sterling thing: but I wished for its representation, and there were so many authors struggling for the same object, that I had not firmness to resist the opportunity that was opened to me through

the kindness of Mr. Macready, to offer it to the proprietor of Covent Garden Theatre. I allowed the
play to appear, whilst I was conscious of its many
shortcomings. The toil of placing a tragedy or
comedy on the stage (apart from the trouble of
writing it), is sufficient to daunt most men from
repeating the experiment. Without doubt, the
activity and kindness of Mr. Macready, and the
general good-will of the actors, saved me from
much trouble and from many rebuffs. The tragedy was acted for sixteen nights; it produced
(including the copyright) 630*l.*; and then passed
away (with other temporary matters) into the
region of the moths. I never attempted to im-
prove or revive it. For my success I was indebted
partly to Mr. Charles Kemble, but principally to
Mr. Macready.

"Dramatic writers have often complained of the
many impediments to a successful issue of their
plays, which spring up behind the curtain of a
theatre. I did not experience any; nor was there
much otherwise to trouble me, beyond the exces-
sive tedium of the rehearsals, and the prosaic
tones in which my tenderest sentences were pronounced. I owed most, without doubt, to the
friendship of Mr. Macready, and much to Mr.

Charles Kemble, to both of whom I was previously known."

It is not often that the first public criticism of a poet's work is the best; and such an early judgment is especially liable to error when it includes a comparison with other and contemporary poetry. But Lord Jeffrey's estimate of " Mr. Cornwall's " writing is probably fuller and juster than anything which has been printed on the subject during the fifty-six years that have since gone by. The following extract from the " Edinburgh " notice of a " Sicilian Story " could scarcely be improved upon :

" Mr. Cornwall's . . . style is chiefly moulded, and his versification modulated, on the pattern of Shakespeare, Marlow, Beaumont and Fletcher, and Massinger. He has also copied something from Milton and Ben Jonson, and the amorous cavaliers of the Usurpation — and then, passing disdainfully over all the intermediate writers, has flung himself fairly into the arms of Lord Byron, Coleridge, Wordsworth, and Leigh Hunt. This may be thought, perhaps, rather a violent transition, and likely to lead to something of an incongruous mixture. But really the materials harmonize very tolerably ; and the candid reader . . . will easily discover the secret of this amalgamation. In the first place, Mr. Cornwall is himself a poet, and one of no mean rate; and, not being a maker of parodies or centos, he does not imitate by indiscriminately caricaturing the prominent peculiarities of his models, or crowding together their external or mechanical characteristics — but merely disciplines his own genius in the school of theirs; and tinges the creatures of his own fancy with the coloring which glows in theirs. In the next place, and what is much more important, it is obvious that a man may imitate Shakespeare and his great compeers without presuming to rival their variety and universality, and merely by endeavoring to copy one or two of their many styles and excellences. This is the case with Mr. Cornwall. He does not meddle with the thunders and lightnings of the mighty poet, and still less with his boundless humor and fresh-springing merriment. . . . It is the tender, the sweet, and the fanciful only that he aspires to copy; the girlish innocence and lovely sorrow of Juliet, Imogen, Perdita, and Viola — the enchanted solitude of Prospero and his daughter — the ethereal loves and jealousies of Oberon and Titania, and those other magical scenes, all perfumed with love and poetry, and breathing the spirit of a celestial spring, which lie scattered in every part of his writings. The genius of Fletcher, perhaps, is more akin to Mr. C.'s muse than the soaring and 'extravagant' spirit of Shakespeare; and we think we can trace . . . the impression which his fancy has received from the patient suffering and sweet desolation of Aspatria, in his 'Maid's Tragedy.' It is the youthful Milton only that he has presumed to copy. . . . From Jonson . . . he has imitated some of those exquisite songs and lyrical pieces which lie buried in the rubbish of his 'Masks.' . . . There is a great deal of the diction of Wordsworth and Coleridge, and some imitation of their beauties; but . . . the natural bent of his genius is more like that of Leigh Hunt than any other author. . . . But he has better taste and better judgment, or, what is perhaps but saying the same thing, he has less affectation and far less conceit. He has scarcely any other affectation, indeed, than is almost necessarily implied in a sedulous imitation of difficult models — and no visible conceit at all. On the contrary, we cannot help supposing him to be a very natural and amiable person, who has taken to write poetry more for the love he bears it, than the fame to which it may raise him; who cares nothing for the

sects and factions into which the poetical world
may be divided, but, regarding himself as a debtor
to any writer who has given him pleasure, desires
nothing better than to range freely over the whole
Parnassian Garden, 'stealing and giving odors'
with a free spirit and a grateful and joyous heart."

In this and other criticisms by Lord Jeffrey, he
dwelt much upon the imitative character of Mr.
Procter's early poems; and the critic was unques-
tionably right.   The young poet's modesty and
enthusiasm, and the occasionally extravagant-lau-
dations of the old English writers by his friends,
Lamb, Hazlitt, and Hunt, led him to regard Nature
and those great interpreters of her as almost equal
powers.   He always, indeed, obeyed the Muse's
prime command, "Look in thy heart, and write,"
but, at this period, he usually paused to mark how
others had written, before trusting his own feelings
and thoughts to verse.   These, however, so far
modified the various ideals of manner which were
adopted by him, that what he wrote had a style of
its own, an elegant, tender, and somewhat con-
sciously childlike, or maiden-like simplicity which
is not quite like anything else in poetry.   A very
pure taste and an excellent ear preserved him
invariably from harshness and coarseness, and fre-

quently enabled him to pour forth strains which surpass, in all essential qualities, much that fashion — as variable and as inscrutable in art as in dress — now pronounces to be high-class poetry. Procter is now known to the public almost exclusively by his songs, some of which have attained the enviable and abiding rank of "Volkslieder." He is the one contradiction of his own assertion that "there is no English song writer of any rank whose songs form the distinguishing feature of his poetry." A good song, however, is made to be sung, and assumes and requires the complement of music, as a good drama does that of acting. For this reason, neither songs nor dramas — meant to be sung or acted — are among the best vehicles for poetry, though, accidentally, the best poetry is often to be found in them. Poetry, as such, includes its own action and its own melody, its scene and its lyre remaining alike the property of the imagination. It is therefore not so much to " Mirandola " and the " English Songs " that we must go for tests of Mr. Procter's poetic character, as to his idyls, the " Sicilian Story," the " Flood of Thessaly," etc., those true eclogues, his " Dramatic Scenes," not written to be acted, and assuming nothing which the reader's imagination is not able

3   D

perfectly to supply, and those of his lyrical poems — not songs — which contain their sufficing music in themselves.

The present generation knows so little of Mr. Procter in his most characteristic functions as a poet, that a few examples of his manner in these kinds will not be out of place. The grace of narrative, which reminds us of several other poets, but which is nevertheless his own, is not more manifest in the opening lines of the " Sicilian Story " than it is throughout that poem and several others.

> One night a masque was held within the walls
> Of a Sicilian palace: the gayest flowers
> Cast life and beauty o'er the marble halls,
> And, in remoter spots, fresh waterfalls
> That rose half hidden by sweet lemon bowers
> A low and silver-voiced music made:
> And there the frail perfuming woodbine strayed,
> Winding its slight arms round the cypress bough,
> And as in female trust seem'd there to grow,
> Like woman's love 'midst sorrow flourishing;
> And every odorous plant and brighter thing
> Born of the sunny skies and weeping rain,
> That from the bosom of the spring
> Starts into life and beauty once again,
> Blossom'd; and there in walks of evergreen,
> Gay cavaliers and dames high-born and fair,
> Wearing that rich and melancholy smile
> That can so well beguile

> The human heart from its recess, were seen,
> And lovers full of love and studious care
> Wasting their rhymes upon the soft night air.

The "Flood of Thessaly," without sacrifice of individuality of style, reminds the reader of Milton and Shakespeare as constantly as the "Sicilian Story" recalls a similar class of narrative by Byron, Shelley, or Leigh Hunt.

>   Apollo's steeds,
> Which wait his coming at the eastern gate,
> Harness'd were there, and champed their crystal bits,
> And threw their flaming foam upon the air.
> Then first, in all its radiant beauty, shone
> The Rainbow, shadowy arch, of every hue
> Of light inwove, in Heaven's immortal loom;
> Gay, rich, illustrious colors mingled there,
> And shone and were involved each within each,
> Atoms of loveliest light, orange and blue,
> Yellow and glowing red and soothing green,
> Lying across the sky.

The now prevailing taste, that demands of the descriptive poet a photographic accuracy and energy of detail, and readily pardons a photographic feebleness and falsehood in the general result, will not be greatly impressed by extracts, which would chiefly prove that Mr. Procter, like most of his famous cotemporaries, considered detail of less consequence than the pervading grace and melodious flow which none but the very greatest poets have been able to secure without some sacrifice of force and exactness in particulars.   His narrative verse abounds, however, with thoughts and images, novel in conception and perfect in expression, which adorn, without checking its musical current.

The " Journal of the Sun " is a fine example of the exercise of that lyrical power which the Poet knew, in later days, to be more peculiarly his own.

Day breaks!   O'er yon bars of deep purple,
  (Cloud-purple,) comes soaring the Dawn;
O'er mountains that lift their black shoulders
  'Twixt Night and the Morn:
And yonder, high-tossing his antlers
  In play or in scorn,
Stands the stag, and beside him outstretching
  His limbs is the fawn.
How lightly he springs o'er the heather!
  How lazily slumber the kine!
How still are the old giant forests!
  And, above, how divine
Is the Sun!   He awakes in a glory:
  His path is array'd
With hues like the flush of the rainbow:
  He scatters the shade —
He has scatter'd the dews and the vapors,
  Where'er he has trod;
And now he uncloudeth his beauty, —
  All over a God.

He moves; — he goes forth on his journey
    From morning to night:
All round him the circle of azure
    Is swimming in light.
Below, all the waters are sparkling;
    All earth is awake:
The lark in the ether is singing,
    The thrush in the brake;
But He hastes, — high away to the zenith;
    Clouds — shadows — they fly:
High, — higher, — he touches, he treads on
.   The arch of the sky!
'Tis Noon!   He outpoureth his splendor:
    The might of his ray   . ·
Strikes dumb the bold Spirits that laugh'd
    In the dawn of the day:
The soldier is conquered; his weapons
    Beside him are laid:
Toil ceases: the horse and his rider
    Are seeking the shade.   .
Doth _he_ pause?   No: already his lustre
    Is far in the West:
But he calms the fierce beams, as he neareth
    The isles of the Bless'd.
Still swift, — like the eagle pursuing
    The falcon in flight, —
He rusheth adown the deep azure,
    Now followed by Night.
Shapes rise from the Ocean to greet him;
    They curtain his bed;
Gold-tinged, like the eye of the topaz;
    Blush-color'd; blood-red;

> Such blue as the amethyst hides
> In the depths of her breast: —
> And thus, — in the bosom of beauty,
> He sinks to his rest.

The following lines from a " fragment " called " Rosamund Gray " contain a singular forecast of an idyllic style which was to be the chief ornament of the poetry of the succeeding half century, and they prove that that which constitutes an essential link in the development of a nation's poetry may fail, for a time at least, to occupy its just place in the nation's memory and gratitude.   These verses and hundreds much like them were published by Mr. Procter in 1820.

> Once — but she died — I knew a village girl
> (Poor Rosamund Gray), who, in my fancy, did
> Surpass the deities you tell me of.
> Haply you may have passed her; and indeed
> Her beauty was not made for all observance,
> If beauty it might be called.   It was a sick
> And melancholy loveliness, that pleased
> But few; and somewhat of its charm, perhaps,
> Owed to the lonely spot she dwelt in.   I
> Knew her from infancy; a shy, sad girl;
> And gossips, when they saw her, oftentimes
> Would tell her future fortunes.   They would note
> Her deep blue eyes, which seemed as they already
> Had made fast friends with sorrow, and could say
> Hers was an early fate.

The popularity of Mr. Procter's narrative and dramatic poems at the time is proved by their appearance in repeated editions; * and the high character of that popularity is no less manifest from the quarters in which his writings were praised and attacked. Laudatory articles of great force and ability, and evident freedom from personal bias, appeared one close upon the other in the " Edinburgh Review ; " and Allibone's " Critical Dictionary of English Literature " indicates no fewer than fourteen articles in " Blackwood's Magazine," in all of which, with one or two exceptions, Mr. Procter's poetry is said to be disparaged. Charles Lamb is known to have declared that " there was not one of the [Dramatic] Fragments to which, had he found them among the Garrick Plays in the British Museum, he would have refused a place in his Dramatic Specimens." Lord Byron, though he indulged, in print, in a somewhat unintelligible sneer at the asserted resemblance of parts of Mr. Procter's poetry to his own, was, in private, as Lady Blessington affirms in her " Conversations " with the lordly poet, a

* The fame of his poetry was not confined to England. Galignani, in 1829, published " The Poetical Works of Milman, Bowles, Wilson, and Barry Cornwall."

great admirer of the poetry of Barry Cornwall, which he says is " full of imagination and beauty, possessing a refinement and delicacy that, whilst they add all the charms of a woman's mind, take off none of the force of a man's."

Miss Martineau, in her short sketch of Mr. Procter, first published in the " Daily News," tells us that " his favorite method was to compose when he was alone in a crowd, and he declared that he did his best when walking London streets." He had " an odd habit of running into a shop to secure his verses, often carrying them away on scraps of crumpled paper in which cheese or sugar had been wrapped."

By very much the most important fruit of the young poet's literary successes, as far as regards himself, was his introduction, in 1820, at the house of Horace Twiss, to Mr. and Mrs. Basil Montagu and Miss Skepper, his future wife, the daughter of Mrs. Montagu by her first marriage. That a poet could hardly have aspired to a greater temporal reward than the friendship of the Basil Montagus and the hand of their daughter will not be questioned by any of the many living persons who have had the happiness of knowing that family. No young man who understood what honor meant —

and none understood it better than the high-minded
and sensitive young poet — could think that fame
had in store for him any favor which could surpass or equal those which she was now conferring·
on him. Hence, perhaps, the sudden and final
extinction of his literary ambition, which seemed
to occur about this time, notwithstanding an
amount of popular encouragement that, under
ordinary circumstances, was calculated to fire him
to redoubled exertions. The manners, at once
stately and genial, of Mr. Basil Montagu and his
wife have few or no counterparts in modern
society. The stateliness was not that of reserve,
but of truth in action, and the geniality arose, not
from easy good humor, but from earnest good
will. Of Mrs. Basil Montagu it may indeed be
said that, for a young man " to know her was an
education." Even at a time when her great personal beauty was slightly (it was never more than
slightly) obscured by age, there was that about her
which no well-disposed and imaginative young
man could long behold without feeling that he
was *committed* thereby to leading a worthy life.
If the reader is inclined to smile at this praise as
somewhat obsolete in its mode, let him be assured

3*

by one who knew Mrs. Montagu that it seems so only because that style of woman is obsolete.

In 1821, the year following Mr. Procter's introduction to this circle, he became engaged to Miss Skepper — whose name, it is interesting to know, was derived lineally from her ancestor, the second in the famous partnership of *Fust and Scheffer*, the earliest printers.   On the 7th of October, 1824, the poet married the lady who by her brilliant qualities made his house one of the chief centres of London literary society for a space of nearly half a century.

The following passages are from Mr. Procter's letters to Miss Skepper:

"I saw Mr. Mackay at Drury Lane last night (he is *very* clever).   I saw the Queen at the Lyceum, and heard Fawcett proclaim at Covent Garden that all the theatres were to be *open gratis* on Thursday night to the public."

" . . . After all, he has, or had when I knew him, some good qualities.   I confess I liked him once very much, and I am sorry to see him so eaten up by pride, which has nothing but station and a title (which, however, Sir W. Curtis shares with him) for its support.   I forswear the bloody hand. My love, I will never be a baronet, no, I am determined; nor a duke, nor any of these vanities. My name shall remain plain Thomson, neither more or less — and yet Lady Cornwall! I hope your ladyship is well? Will you go out to-day, my lady? These things sound harmoniously."

"I have promised Mr. Richardson to dine with him on Saturday, to meet Joanna Baillie and a sister of Mrs. Jeffrey, etc. I shall not set off till five o'clock, and shall probably be back at half-past nine, although I do not expect you will return so soon. I was hesitating what to say to Mr. Richardson, till I recollected your injunctions about going to see him, and reflected that I had already neglected his kind advances."

"I have just a letter from the Secretary of the New Literary Institution in Waterloo Place (the Athenæum), saying that I have been elected a member, and requesting me to send ten guineas and the entrance fee of five." *

"I am better to-day. What do you think of

* He was one of the hundred members who were originally elected; but he declined, being about to be married.

Charles Lamb (it was after supper) saying to his company, among whom was Wordsworth and his train. ' We sit ve-ve-ve-e-ry silent here. Like a company in a parlor — all silent and all damned.' "

" I send you the ' Bride's Tragedy.' It contains more promise (without any exception) than any first work I ever saw — beyond Keats and everbody else, I think."

" I went to the Haymarket to see the ' Alcaide.' I left Miss Paton trilling away like a drummer's fife, and Madame Vestris in pantaloons as lively as ever ; Liston hideous as usual ; Mr. Glover as big as a butt of sherry ; and Farren (the Alcaide) as self-sufficient and foolish even as an English justice, but perhaps a little more good-natured."

" By-the-bye, in the ' Fall of Saturn,' it should be the *track* and not the *grave* of the pale twilight. The grave, I am afraid, is stationary.

" You see what small rocks scribblers of rhyme and writers of metaphor may split upon. Our Charybdis may be in a monosyllable — a poor thing, no more than a ' hem,' yet we may be wrecked. Pity us, my sweet Anne, but above all

pity me (the unworthiest of the tribe), and love
me at least twenty times beyond my deserts."

" How did you, my dearest, get to Chertsey (not
to Whitefriars) ?   What were your companions
like ?   Was the man with the long nose as inno-
cent as his looks proclaimed ?   I rely on the man
(or woman) with crutches, and I have small fears
about the young woman or lady.   I have nothing
to tell you about Blackheath.   The leaves are sere
— red, brown, and yellow, and now and then one
looks like green ; yet I am ungrateful, for there is
a fir just opposite my window with dull-green
prickly leaves and black boughs, that seems to
reproach me for forgetting its summer neighbors ;
and even the party-colored leaves are pleasant
enough, and the odor of the fallen ones delightful.
It surpasses (in its associations) even the scents
of April itself, or rather May, for we look at April
only and scent May.   I have not been into the
park yet, though perhaps I may before tea.   But
the walls look bare enough, and there are no
embossed trees hanging their green heads over it.
I see nothing but a wilderness of stripped dark
little branches shooting up above the long length
of brick."

" I perceive that I am writing a very stupid letter, my dear girl, but the fact is that I can't stoop very well over the table (this is like the accountant, who, making a mistake in the casting, laid the blame on his bad pen), and my ideas do not flow so rapidly through a crooked as through a straight channel. Ah, I am making mistakes, dear, you see ; for I am straighter than ever — more upright. Perhaps it is the stiffness which destroys my wit and cramps it. Dispose of the matter as you please. Lay the blame on anything but yourself, and I am content."

" Will your friend give me some blanc-mange ? but no, I don't like blanc-mange. I hate nothing but green tea, and my enemies, and insincerity, and affectation, and undue pretence. It is partly, I believe, because you have none of these, that I love you so much."

" Well, I dined with Mr. Kean, and what little I saw of him I liked much. He seems very pleas- ant and good-natured and unaffected; yet his features are much altered, I think for the worse. They speak of festivity and such matters, I fear, too plainly. He knew me. I told him I had been

introduced to him, and he said, ' By the Montagus,
I believe ; ' but I said, ' No, by some one in Drury
Lane green-room.'   We talked of Dr. Drury, Lord
Byron, etc.   He did not stay long, being obliged
to act Richard III.   He is going to America again.
He seems not to like Elliston, and to think that
going to Covent Garden will be prejudicial to him,
as (he thinks) acting with Young has been at
Drury Lane ; yet surely this is a fancy."

The " Flood of Thessaly " was dedicated to
Miss Skepper in verses which abound in beauty,
though the poet's imaginative passion is expressed
with so much classical imagery and allusion, that
most modern readers will prefer the pieces written
by " The Poet to his Wife," many years after.

At this time Mr. Procter was a constant play-
goer.   He seldom missed an evening, and used to
say that he felt as if the day was not properly
finished unless he had looked in at Drury Lane or
Covent Garden.   Before and behind the curtains
of these theatres he used to meet many literary
friends, who, like himself, were the constant
devotees of the dramatic muses, then at the
height of the glory from which they were
destined to pass, through a quarter of a century

of decline, into almost utter degradation and neglect.

About this time the poet seems to have been solicited by Mr. (afterwards Lord) Jeffrey to contribute regularly to the " Edinburgh Review." Mr. Procter, it appears, promised several articles, but only wrote two or three. Of these pieces he thought very little, and spoke afterwards of one of them — a sort of general survey of English poetry — in a letter to Mr. Fields, as " written hastily, — very imperfect, — by no means coming up to my idea of the subject at that time, and very far below it now." This essay appears to have been written during the later days of the poet's bachelorhood, and under constant pressure from the great " editor " to get it finished. It bears the marks of interfering forces, and is, of all the pieces republished in the American collection of Mr. Procter's prose, the least finished in thought and style.

He wrote about or soon after this time many prose pieces, most of which were " occasional." Some were contributions, made perhaps at the solicitation of friends, to " Annuals," which, forty or fifty years ago, formed no contemptible portion of the then current literature, the greatest names

of the time appearing among the contributors to
" Keep-sakes " and " Forget-me-nots." Several
essays of a more serious character, chiefly on poets
and poetry, appeared in Reviews and as introduc-
tions to editions of Shakespeare, Ben Jonson, etc.
Messrs. Ticknor and Fields published a collection
of some of these shorter pieces, in two volumes,
entitled " Essays and Tales in Prose. By Barry
Cornwall " (Boston, U.S., 1853). The " Tales "
are usually pieces of consummate form, and,
though few and brief, contain abundant proof
that their writer had in him the making of an
excellent novelist. The criticisms, though full of
acute and important remarks, have a somewhat
cursory and unsystematic character, such as might
be expected of a writer who was too good a poet
to make a patient investigator of the method of
his art. The short " Defence of Poetry " is of
more personal interest than the rest, as showing
how much and how well its author had considered
the moral " raison-d'être " of poetry as the great
means — to use Lord Bacon's words — of " apply-
ing and commending the dictates of reason to the
imagination, for the better moving of the appetite
and the will." He says wittily of Plato that " he
denied admittance to a poet in his ideal republic ;

E

and his republic has remained ideal." Against the sceptics as to the " use " of poetry, he writes, " After all, poetry is no more a fiction than are certain maxims of law and state, which have been engrafted on the severest and most practical of the sciences, in order the better to enforce or illustrate some of their most important doctrines. Nor is it more a delusion — even when it holds up a picture of. ideal excellence — than any prose Atlantis or Utopia which has been devised for practical and direct imitation. Nay, might not the same charge be brought against any scheme of moral and political good, which might be drawn out for the benefit of mankind at the present moment — a state of things desirable, it may be, for a moralist or legislator, but as utterly unadapted, *in its whole extent*, as poetry itself, to the passions and affections of human nature? There is not a single comfort that we enjoy which is not liable to this imputation (of uselessness).

> Our basest beggars
> Are in the poorest things superfluous."

And he adds, with admirable brevity and weight, " If life itself were not a pleasure, the utility even of its necessaries might very well be questioned."

After his marriage, Mr. Procter returned in earnest to the profession for which he had been trained. He began as a conveyancer, and received his first business from his old friend Mr. John Jenkyns, of 14, Red Lion Square; the home of the poet and his wife being at this time the upper part of a house in Southampton Row. Work rapidly increased upon him, and he gave such a hearty welcome to it that it was his habit, at this time, to sit up, on an average, two entire nights a week. His wife has written, " I do not think that any literary successes ever gratified him so much as when some solicitor on the adverse side, pleased with his work, employed him." He now took pupils, of whom he had between forty and fifty. Amongst these were Mr. A. W. Kinglake and Mr. Eliot Warburton, afterwards his life-long friends. In 1825 the young married pair went to live with Mr. and Mrs. Basil Montagu, 25, Bedford Square, where the poet's first child, Adelaide, was born. Here they remained for several years, singularly happy, if to have " troops of friends," a fair competence, a rising family of extraordinary promise, and *no history*, is to be happy.

In a letter to Mr. James T. Fields, many years later, Mr. Procter writes : —

" I wish that I had, when younger, made more notes about my contemporaries; for being of no faction in politics, it happens that I have known far more literary men than any other person of my time. In counting up the names of persons known to me who were, in some way or other, *connected* with literature, I reckoned up more than one hundred. But then I had more than sixty years to do this in. My first acquaintance of this sort was Bowles, the poet. This was about 1805."

This idea of writing some account of his more famous contemporaries seems to have dwelt in the poet's mind for many years, before he at last seriously, in his old age, set about its realization. In the year 1828, however, he began to make a few notes, journal-wise, in this direction. The delicate, strong, and unsuperfluous " touch " of these early delineations must make every reader of them regret, with the author, that he did not execute more of them while his memories were fresh, and his hand was in its highest power.

The following memoranda, concerning the Kembles, Cooper the novelist, Sir Thomas Lawrence, George Dyer, Campbell, and Stothard, are all that remain of Mr. Procter's early notes in this kind.

[*No Date.*]

" . . . It was thus that I became acquainted with the great histrionic family of Kembles. John Kemble (whom I saw only once, in private) had retired to Lausanne; but I was once or twice in the company of Mrs. Siddons, and I may venture to say that I was intimate with Mr. and Mrs. Charles Kemble, and their accomplished daughters, and I saw something of their two sons. Of this family, I think that Mrs. Charles Kemble was the most active minded (although all her children were more than clever). I found her very ready and amiable in conversation, and capable of talking almost on any subject. She spoke French fluently and well (she was indeed of French descent); she was sufficiently well read in general literature, and was a practical woman of the world. Being of a quick temper, she was not so universally liked as she deserved. When I first made the acquaintance of this family, Mr. and Mrs. Kemble lived in Gerrard Street, afterwards in Soho Square, and finally at or near Chertsey, where she had a cottage, and died somewhat suddenly and before she had time to grow old. Her eldest son gained some distinction as a Saxon scholar; her eldest daughter was a good (and very energetic) tragic actress, and her youngest became an accomplished singer : they were all remarkably able.   The excellences of Charles Kemble as an actor are, I believe, generally admitted.   He was not good in tragedy (in which he was artificial), but his comedy was superlative.   He was capital in ' Cassio,' ' Mercutio,' ' Charles Surface,' and other parts ; but best of all in ' Mirabel ' in ' The Inconstant,' in which his acting (which ultimately became tragic and fearful) exceeded everything that I have seen, except the most brilliant points in Edmund Kean's best characters.

" From the Kembles to the suave Sir Thomas Lawrence the transition seems natural.   This gentleman was a great admirer of all the Kemble family.   He was fond of talking of them, and of painting them in their various stage characters. I saw Sir T. Lawrence first at a dinner of Mr. C. Kemble's in Gerrard Street.   Mrs. Siddons was there eating and drinking amongst the mortals, and uttering a few ordinary words in grave, perhaps solemn tones.   Her ' I will take a slice of mutton, if you please,' would have become Lady Macbeth.   It was listened to with awe.   Nevertheless there was nothing affected in her tone or manner, which was merely serious from habit.   I saw her perform in all her famous stage characters, and she was unutterably the greatest tragic actress whom I have seen on the English stage.

"Of Sir T. Lawrence I afterwards saw a good deal. He was a great collector of old drawings, which I was at that time accustomed to search for throughout the whole of London. I have traversed almost all the streets and alleys of the city during my inquiries for these pieces of art. In the course of my peregrinations I succeeded in picking up some choice specimens of Dominichino, Fra Bartolomeo, and even Raffaelle. My best (and it was an undoubted drawing of Raffaelle) I parted with to Sir T. Lawrence, in return for which he was to paint a portrait of my (then intended) wife. Unluckily he died before he commenced the picture.

"If the plan proposed to myself in these Recollections included actors instead of literary men, I could set forth at great length all that I saw of Edmund Kean, of whom I was a great admirer. I saw him act in all his great characters, and afterwards wrote a life of him, which was published by Mr. Moxon in 1832. The materials from which this biography was drawn were furnished by his widow, and were very scanty. There was no

great willingness and little trouble manifested in
disinterring circumstances which troubled his early
career. He was a great — or rather he was a
brilliant actor; in certain scenes or passages
second to none. His acting appeared to be the
result of inspiration rather than of steady or severe
study; and in some of his characters this inspiration failed. In ' Richard ' and ' Othello ' he was
at his greatest excellence. In parts of ' Macbeth '
and of ' Sir Giles Overreach,' and even of ' Hamlet,' he was very brilliant; but in ' Lear ' and
other great characters, which were only to be conquered by great study and exertion (he having no
great aptitude for those parts), his success was
certainly doubtful. The beauty and spirit of particular scenes or passages were not in themselves
sufficient to encircle the whole with glory.

"Kean's excellence and defects have excited
great disputes amongst the critics, each of whom
has chosen to examine only one side of the shield.
His private has been imported into his public life,
and this has enlarged and perplexed the controversy. In cases of this sort, we should be content
to accept the good and the doubtful together, the
personal with the intellectual qualities. We do
not know how inextricably the two are inter-

mixed. The dash and decision of strong opinions may depend in some degree, perhaps, on the impatience with which they are made up in the mind of the writer. We cannot ascertain with unerring precision upon what grounds any man's opinion is formed. He probably looks at the object which he professes to describe from a different point to that occupied by yourself; and the impetus with which his sentences are emitted (and which frequently constitutes their merit) would have been lost if his patience had served him so as to examine microscopically every detail.

"In the case of Edmund Kean, there is some doubt whether, if he had been a careful explorer of all the shades which distinguish the light and darkness of Shakespeare's creations, he might not have failed in marking with all the vivid energy that he exhibited the ' Richard ' and ' Othello ' of our unapproachable poet."

"*Saturday, May,* 1828.

"Mrs. Charles Kemble called here to-day, and among other things told us a strange story of an occurrence to which her husband was witness at Brussels. It was as follows : — Some years ago Mr. Charles Kemble on entering Brussels found

4

that there was preparation making for an execution that occupied a good deal of attention. Three men were to be executed; but one man was remarkable for having committed almost twenty assassinations — having broken prison, etc., and for being a person of remarkable talent. Mr. Kemble determined to witness the spectacle. Now it is to be observed that at Brussels they do not (or did not) execute any criminals after a certain hour in the day; and in order not to run too near this hour, the culprits are taken to the block some considerable time beforehand. The two undistinguished rogues were melancholy enough; but the notorious one was anything but chap-fallen. He was well dressed, had a good carriage, hummed (I believe) a popular air, and in all other things exhibited the extreme of self-possession. On his way to the guillotine (or when he arrived there) he said, 'Now don't mix my head with those fellows; keep me apart. I would not have it supposed that I had such a rascally look as either of those vagabonds for the world ' — or to this effect."

" *May* 17*th*, 1828.

" I met this evening (for the first time) with Cooper, the American writer. He is the author of the 'Pioneers,' the 'Spy,' etc. He has a dogged, discontented look, and seems ready to affront or to be affronted. His eye is rather deep-set, dull, and with little motion. One might imagine that he had lost his life in gazing at seas and woods and rivers, and that he would gaze — gaze on for ever. His conversation is rough, abrupt, and unamusing ; yet I am told that he can recount an adventure well, and I can easily believe it. There was something peculiar in his physiognomy, but I could not make out what it was. I told Mrs. M—— that he seemed to me as though he ought to have had a pigtail (of hair) at the back of his head. She replied that she thought it was because he bore some resemblance to Captain Cook, whose portrait with a pigtail I had been used to see. But that was not it. I afterwards recollected a peculiar motion and rolling of the mouth, as though he chewed tobacco. The fact was that he had the look of a sailor ; which neither the character of author or 'travelled' gentleman could hide. He was once, I believe, mate of an Indiaman (an *American* Indiaman), and had brought the habits of his old life — rudeness and all — into the civilized society of Europe. Cooper was invited to dine at the Duke of Devonshire's, but he was affronted because the Duke had not called upon him. I forget whether he went or not; but I believe he did.

"He went to Lord Spencer's. At dinner he did not take anything; and on Lady S. inquiring whether hē would not eat, he replied that 'He expected the dishes to be brought round to him.' Lady Spencer said that this was not the custom here. He answered that it was the custom at Paris. As he had been in England three times before, and had passed the greater part of his life at sea and in America, and only eighteen months in France, the lady felt a little surprised at his expectations, and asked him if the last twelve months of his life had effaced all his old impressions. I forgot what answer he made, but he deported himself very bluffly and disagreeably. He resembles very much a caricature that I remember to have seen indicative of 'Damme, who cares?'

"Cooper was also at Lord Holland's. When there, Lady H. (who had heard that he told some story about a whale or a shark very well) turned the conversation upon his adventure. 'I believe, Mr. Cooper, that *you* have sustained some perils of this kind?' (the talk had previously been about

marine monsters — under board and *a*-board).
Cooper replied, 'Yes.' — 'Your adventure was
with a whale?' — 'No; a shark.' — 'Had you a
narrow escape?' — 'Yes.' — 'Pray how was it?'
— 'I've told the story before, — to those two;'
and he pointed to Rogers and another gentleman,
who were at table. He should be put in a cage,
and taught civil tunes; or he will grow as bad as
the vert-vert, who came back to the nuns of the
Visitation with oaths in his mouth big enough to
frighten an abbess.

"Cooper was complimented here upon his
books. He was assured that they were much
admired in England and had had a 'great run.'
They had 'pleased the English,' etc. 'It wasn't
what I intended, then,' replied he of the Ohio.
He seems to have 'meant nothing but fighting,'
as they say in the ring.

"*May* 17, 1828.

"Poor George Dyer — whom Lamb has celebrated — formed one subject of conversation this
evening. He invited some one — I think it was
Llanos, the author of 'Esteban' and 'Sandoval'
— to breakfast with him one day in Clifford's Inn.
Dyer of course forgot all about the matter very

speedily after giving the invitation; and when
Llanos went at the appointed hour, he found
nothing but little Dyer, and his books and his dust
— the work of years — at home.   George, however, was anything but inhospitable, as far as his
means or ideas went; and on being told that
Llanos had come to breakfast, proceeded to inves-
tigate his cupboard.   He found the remnant of a
threepenny loaf, two cups and saucers, a little
glazed teapot, and a spoonful of milk.   They sat
down, and (Dyer putting the hot water into the
teapot) commenced breakfast.   Llanos attacked the
stale crust, which Lazarillo de Tomes himself would
have despised, and waited with much good humor
and patience for his tea.   At last, out it came.
Dyer, who was half blind, kept pouring out —
nothing but hot water from the teapot, until
Llanos, who thought a man might be guilty of too
much abstinence, inquired if D. had not forgot *the
tea.*   ' God bless me ! ' replied D., ' and so I have.'

" He began immediately to remedy his error,
and emptied the contents of a piece of brown paper
into the teapot, deluged it with water, and sat
down with a look of complete satisfaction.   ' How
very odd it was that I should make such a mistake ! ' said Dyer.   However, he now determined

to make amends, and filled Llanos' cup again. Llanos thought the tea had a strange color, but not having dread of aqua tofana before his eyes, he thrust his spoon in and tasted. It was *ginger!* Seeing that it was in vain to expect commonplaces from the little absentee, Llanos continued cutting and crumbling a little bread into his plate for a short time and then departed. He went straight to a coffee-house in the neighborhood, and was just finishing a capital breakfast when Dyer came in, to read the paper, or to inquire after some one who frequented the coffee-house. He recognized Llanos, and asked him how he did ; but felt no surprise at seeing him devouring a second breakfast. He had totally forgotten all the occurrences of the morning.

" It was in reference to Dyer's spare commons that Lamb re-christened his dog. Dyer had a dog whose name was Tobit ; Lamb called him *No*-bit.

" I happened to call at Lamb's the morning that Dyer fell into the New River. He had been taken out about a quarter of an hour when I arrived, and I saw the track of water from the river to the house, which was close by, like that left by a large Newfoundland dog. I rang the bell. 'Is Mr. Lamb at home ?' I inquired. — 'No, sir,' answered the maid, 'but Mr. Dyer has just fallen into the water; *will* you go up? My Missis is in such a fright.' I proceeded accordingly up-stairs, and there found Dyer blanketed up to the throat; his little stubby gray hair had been rubbed up till it looked like a quantity of little needles on his head. He was chattering away under the influence of a thundering glass of brandy-and-water; while Miss Lamb was standing by the bedside, diving and plunging into the pockets of his wet trousers for his keys, money, etc. 'Poor Mr. Dyer!' said she, whimpering. 'He has had such an accident' — 'Oh, I'm very well now,' replied he. 'But it certainly was *very* extraordinary; I really thought it was the path. I walked on and on, and suddenly — I was in. But I soon found where I was,' added he. — 'I should think so,' said I; to which Dyer answered, 'Oh, yes.' I left him to the care of Miss Lamb and a sort of itinerant doctor with one eye, who lodged at the public-house hard by. He prescribed nothing but cognac. I suppose for the benefit of the house."

" *June* 1st, 1828.

" Mr. Wrangham breakfasted at Rogers's some mornings ago, and learned there that Campbell —

the poet — had lost his wife.　Mr. W. heard that
Campbell had mentioned that some pigeons which
frequented his house deserted the place soon after
his wife fell ill, and have never since returned.
On the day of her death, in the place of the
pigeons which had flown away, and which were a
blue or gray or some such color, came two pigeons
perfectly milk-white, and settled on her bedroom
window.　After remaining there some time —
much longer than is usual with birds where there
are persons moving to and fro in a room — they
also flew off.　She expressed a wish that they
should return; 'But although I cannot have them,
I have *you*,' she said, turning to her husband.　In
a minute or two afterwards she died."

"*June*, 1828.

"Last summer I and my wife and Mrs. Montagu
went to Sir Thomas Lawrence's one evening, to
look over his old drawings.　He received us with
civility and coffee.　He inquired what drawings
we would look at.　Mrs. Montagu said, 'Michael
Angelo.'　I, who had seen the M. Angelo drawings before, said 'Raffaelle.'　So we each sat down
to our feast of art, Sir Thomas standing by, telling
the story of each, or narrating anecdotes of dif-

4*　　　　　　　　F

ferent persons, with whom he and Mrs. M. were mutually acquainted. Mrs. M. handled the drawings very tenderly, knowing that Sir Thomas was somewhat particular about them, and seeing, indeed, that his method of keeping and mounting them savored somewhat of the finical. He had given each of us an ivory paper-knife to turn over the silver paper which covered each drawing, and Mrs. Montagu was insinuating this like a probe between the paper and the drawing. Perceiving that she did this very carefully (as might be expected), the President spoke to her encouragingly — ' Be bold,' said he; and she proceeded accordingly. As for me, I used less ceremony about the Raffaelle sketches. I had been a buyer and possessor of drawings myself, and treated them like reasonable curiosities. Sir Thomas kept them as the friars do their relics — the rope of Saint Francis, or the tip of the nail of St. Dominic.

" During the evening Sir Thomas told us of his having been taken once to visit a female of extreme beauty. A friend of his wished him as an artist to see, and if possible take a study of, this woman. He went accordingly and saw her. She was, he said, most exquisitely beautiful, perhaps more so than any person he had ever seen : but the eye of an artist is quick at detecting faults, and he saw lurking, among her perfections, or rather peeping out from among them occasionally, an expression which was diabolical. He did not like her. Whether he took any sketch or not he did not say; but, he added, that he learned afterwards that 'the lady' went to live with a young man, whom she entirely ruined. When in great distress, from her extravagance, she induced him to commit forgery; and when he was taken up for the crime, she appeared and volunteered her evidence against him; *and upon her evidence he was hanged.* Here was a beauty!

"I think this Millwood lived somewhere in Devonshire; and that it was there that Sir Thomas saw her."

STOTHARD.

"*August* 16, 1828.

"I went this day to Stothard's the painter. We looked over some of his sketches and prints, and etchings from his designs. He seems to pique himself more upon his correctness than on anything else, and says nothing about the grace of his figures. 'I was very correct,' said he, showing me a somewhat uninteresting pencil sketch of part of Edinburgh. 'This was done from the window of the house where I lodged. It is all correct. I was particular as to that. See, this house had one, two,' — etc., — 'twelve stories; and here,' etc., detailing the course of the streets and wynds one after another. He showed me some of his sketches, in oil, for parts of the dome of the Advocates' Library at Edinburgh. 'I painted Apollo in the middle, and the Nine Muses (each in a compartment) round.'

"'Did you see Sir Walter Scott or Mr. Jeffrey,' inquired I, 'when you were there?'

"'Yes; I saw them both. Mr. Jeffrey spoke to me; but Sir Walter did not. I intended to have put him into my picture, but they would not allow it.'

"'How was that?' asked I.

"'Why, sir, there are, you see, two parties at Edinburgh, who are on bad terms with each other; and I received my instructions from a partisan of the opposite faction, if I may so call it. I put some of the poets in one department of my picture, and filled up some vacant spaces with little boys flying along with garlands to crown them (which I thought a good idea). Well, I put in Shakespeare and Milton — and, as it was in Scotland, I put in

Burns. I wished to put in Sir Walter Scott, as I told you, but Lord Eldon would not permit me.'

" ' Lord Eldon ! ' said I. ' What could tempt him to meddle in such a matter ? '

" ' I received all my instructions from him,' was the reply ; ' and when I proposed it, he objected, and said, " We don't think a tenth part so much of Sir Walter Scott here as you do in England." So I was obliged to submit.'

" ' But Lord Eldon,' said I, ' is our Lord Chancellor *here* — in England. I can't conceive what he could have to do with Edinburgh. If it had been Newcastle-upon-Tyne, indeed —— '

" ' Well,' answered Stothard, ' I don't know whether the name is Eldon, or Elgin — or what ; but the person I mean was John Clerk, the advocate. He was son of that Clerk that wrote a book on naval affairs, which Rodney made his study and followed.'

" We afterwards talked upon the subject of Burleigh, where he painted the great staircase, etc. ' How long did it occupy you ? ' said I.

" ' Why, sir,' returned S——, ' I went down there only during the summer months. I was there four summers (for three or four months each summer), and I received for each visit 300*l*., that

is, 1200*l.* in all.   A Mr. Carey, who has written
something about it, states that I was occupied four
years upon it (which was wrong) ; that I received
300*l.*, while in truth I received 1200*l.*   He should
have inquired of me the fact, before he printed
such a misstatement.'

" ' How long is it ago since you did the painting
at Burleigh ? '

" ' I forget the exact year,' said S——; 'but
this' (pointing to an oil sketch in the room, which
had a sort of Rubens look; it was called the
' Triumph of Intemperance,' I think), this was
painted in 1802, and see how this blue has stood.
I painted this with Prussian blue now — let me
see — six and twenty years ago, and it has not
flown in the least.   Now this ' (added he, turning
to a picture of Venus and Cupid with the Three
Graces), 'all this distance is touched over with
ultramarine.'

" ' What colors have you used,' said I, ' in the
bodies of those Three Graces?   The flesh is excel-
lently done.   I don't myself like those *very* fleshy
figures — for instance, some of Rubens' — they
remind me of the butchers' shambles.   How did
you color this ? '

" *S.* ' I used red ochre and yellow ochre — a little

vermilion, and I put in these shadows with bone brown.'

" *P.* 'You do not use many colors, I believe ? '

" *S.* 'Very few — a good many reds.   In water colors I put in most of my shadows with lake.'

" *P.* ' The shadows of the flesh, I suppose ? '

" *S.* ' Yes ; and sometimes of the drapery.'

" *P.* 'Do you use Indian ink ? '

" *S.* 'Sometimes.   It is a very good color.   I very often mix lake and Indian ink for the shadows of my flesh.   Look! you see I have this morning been using all these reds ; ' and he turned and pointed to six or seven little dishes, all of which had had reds of different shades rubbed in them.

" We afterwards looked over some prints and etchings after his designs, when the following conversation occurred : —

" *P.* 'You must have seen a great many changes of costume ?   The draperies in your early designs are now quite antiquated.   How long is it since you made the designs for the " Novelist's Magazine " ? '

" *S.* 'I forget; my memory is very bad.   I was obliged to look over some letters this morning to ascertain when I went to Burleigh and Edinburgh, etc.   But as to the designs, I did not follow

the fashion of the time exactly. The ladies wore
hoops then, and I took the liberty of striking off
the hoop. These engravings went to France
afterwards ; and I was told that the French,
partly from seeing my designs of English ladies
(not *wholly*, mind you, but *partly*), gave up their
hoops, and then *we* followed the example of the
French.'

" *P.* ' Do these designs on wood cost you much
trouble, or time ? '

" *S.* ' Sometimes. I am obliged to be very particular.'

" *P.* ' I like this sort of engraving, if I may so
call it. I like all painters' etchings ; I am sure of
having what the painter has done. Whereas in
prints (with exceedingly few exceptions) I am
sure of having what the painter has *not* done.
Half the engravers cannot draw, and yet they
engrave ! Do you find them tolerably faithful ? '

" *S.* ' Pretty well. I don't complain.'

" *P.* ' It is of no use, I suppose ? '

" *S.* ' I don't complain. One can't expect them
to be so true as one's own pen. They have not
made it their study ; and *I* have.'

" *P.* ' You studied a good deal from the naked
figure, I suppose, as well as from the antique ? '

" *S.* ' Yes ; I studied very hard at outline.   An outline ought to express everything that a painter wants.   The color and shadows only make it round and so forth.   Many years ago I had a friend whose sight was bad, and did not allow him to look at pictures from a distance ; so he studied outline, and copied from the antique — from vases, etc.   I saw what depended on outline ; and so I went to the Academy, where I studied, with a pen and ink only.   I had no pencil, and couldn't rub out, and so I was obliged to be very careful.   This practice gave me a power of drawing and a facility that I found of great advantage.'

" *P.* ' Outline is a great thing, certainly — the first thing, beyond doubt, for we see what Raffaelle has done with scarcely anything else.   But I am nevertheless very fond of color.   Titian, Correggio, and Giorgione appear to me to be very fine in their way — to say nothing of their grace or expression, I mean — their color and roundness (the latter more particularly in reference to Correggio) are very captivating.'

" *S.* ' Certainly.   I was studying a picture of Titian's the other day at — at Pall Mall — at the exhibition there — what is it ? '

" *P.* ' You mean the British Institution ; the old

masters are exhibited there at present. Did you
see many that you liked ? '

" *S.* ' Not many.   I was studying a picture by
Titian of a female — they call it his daughter;
but I don't think that it is his daughter, probably
his mistress.   I was studying the texture and so
forth of it.   I like to see how those painters
worked.   But I saw little in the exhibition to my
fancy.   I saw nothing that I liked so much, or
thought so good, as your large picture — the
Correggio.'

" *P.* ' Which ? the female ? '

" *S.* ' Yes ; the female.   I forget the other.   The
one I mean is a virgin or an angel.   I thought it
very fine.   I have often thought of it since.   I
forget all your pictures but that.'

" *P.* ' Don't you remember the Giorgione ? '

" *S.* ' No.   I have quite forgot it.' "

In connection with the foregoing account of
Stothard, the great resemblance between him and
Mr. Procter may be noted.   In their characters,
even more than in their works, there is a quality
rarely found elsewhere, except in sensitive, single-
hearted (and slightly " spoilt ") children ; children
who are confident of their company, and have not

been laughed or frightened out of knowing and speaking their own minds. These alone express themselves with such directness, concreteness, and naive limitation; often attaining, in their artlessness, to humor, wit, and grace, which are the artist's envy. The greatest point of resemblance between Stothard and the poet is that last named — a narrow limitation of the sphere of thought and feeling; a sort of voluntary ignoring of all that might clash with or contradict the habitual mood or idea. This habit of soul gave rise, in Mr. Procter, to certain peculiar antipathies and partialities. He loved few mental prospects in which the horizons were hazy, even though the haziness were the legitimate result of remoteness. Hence, probably, his feeling about Coleridge and De Quincey, of whom he commonly spoke and wrote with a sense of their defects of character which was not softened, as it was in the case of Hazlitt and others, by sympathy with their intellectual aims and views.

Stothard and Mr. Procter are alike chargeable with sometimes giving an effect of hard outlines where no outlines really exist; and this through no incapacity of touch, but by an artistic idiosyncrasy, an insistence on the beloved limitations, a

protest against the vastness, variety, and inscruta-
bility of fact.   In many of the " English Songs "
the   sentiments   are   in   flagrant   and   conscious
opposition to " political " and other " economies,"
which are nothing but systematized statements of
natural conditions.   In *life*, however, the poet had
his footing well upon the world of good sense, and
his favorite advice, to people who were free of
their money, to beware lest, in endeavoring to
relieve the poor, they were only relieving the
payers of poor-rates, is in entire opposition to his
poetic philanthropy.   It was the same with his
views of men.   Miss Martineau suggests, with, it
is to be hoped, a somewhat unjust assumption concerning the class to which she herself belonged,
that " it is probable that his distrust of human
nature and character — his judgment of the world
— was formed from the world he knew best. . . .
His house was one of the centres of the literary
world, and he judged men generally by those he
knew."   To suppose that Mr. Procter's actual
views of men are to be taken from his poetry,
would be as much an error as it would be to put
him down as the greatest of topers, because he
wrote more and better drinking songs than any
one else ; or to conclude that he was without

religion because he most frequently took the simple and picturesque view of death that best suited his style of art:

> A flower above, and the mould below;
> And this is all that the mourners know.

His dark views of mankind, in general, were little more than the means of poetic *chiaroscuro;* and the frequent flashings of his scorn, to quote his own words, about somebody else, are but

> Innocuous lightnings, unallied to thunder,

having as little relation to his actual feelings as had the famous song, " The sea, the sea " — which, the only time he was ever on it, made him very sick. In a letter to his friend, Mr. J. T. Fields, he says: " I believe that the best mode of making one's way to a person's head is — through his heart." That is not the creed of a misanthrope, but rather of the man concerning whom the same friend writes: " Who that ever came habitually into his presence, can forget the tones of his voice, the tenderness in his gray retrospective eyes, or the touch of his sympathetic hand laid on the shoulder of a friend ! The elements were, indeed, so kindly mixed in him, that no bitterness, or rancor, or jealousy, had part or lot in his composition.

No distinguished person was ever more ready to help forward the rising, and as yet nameless, literary man or woman who asked his counsel and warm-hearted suffrage.   His mere presence was sunshine and courage to a new-comer into the growing world of letters. . . . Indeed, to be *human* only entitled anyone who came near him to receive the gracious bounty of his goodness and courtesy.   He made it the happiness of his life never to miss, whenever opportunity occurred, the chance of conferring pleasure and gladness on those who needed kind words and substantial aid." *

Mr. Procter was called to the bar in 1831, and in 1832 he closed his career as a poet, by publishing the " English Songs."   In this year he accepted the office of Metropolitan Commissioner of Lunacy. This period of his life was also marked by the loss of his second son, Edward, who died in his sixth year.   The father's grief is recorded in the following touching verses, which he never printed :

* " ' Barry Cornwall ' and some of his Friends.   By James T. Fields."   In " Harper's New Monthly Magazine."

EDWARD, MY SON.

DIED IN HIS 6TH YEAR.

For evermore — for ever, *evermore*
Lies he within thine arms, O mother Earth!
Then clasp him to thee, gently, — with thy soft
And tenderest folding — for he was the best
And dearest (unto me) in all the world!
He was my own — O, in familiar love
How often have I told him thus, and pressed
His head against my heart, caressing it.
For but to touch him was a sweet delight —
To look on him — to know that he was near,
And well, and full of careless happiness.

———

Sickness is in our house, and pain and woe
(Pain of the inmost heart— unending woe)
And Death has come — and gone!   He leaves no track —
None — but a frightful void, which change, nor time,
Nor prosperous days
Can ever again refill.   A little time
And we were happy.   In our cheerful room
(From which the light has fled) we looked around
And saw bright faces, and heard happy words —
Some still remain: but he, whose look was bright
Beyond the rest, and on whose " pretty tongue "
Hung tender accents that were dear to us,
And sweeter than all music — where is he?
Our best and best belovèd, — Dead and gone!

———

My best beloved, hast thou fled,
    And left me — me who loved thee so,
(Who loves thee still — though cold and dead)
    Beyond what thou didst ever know?

They tell me that I made thee, Dear,
　Mine idol, breaking God's great law:
If so, I pay, with bitter tear,
　For errors that I never saw!

They say that earth is filled with flowers,
　That mine may be a happy lot,
That life is rich in sunny hours,
　It may be — but I see them not.

I only see a little shape
　That used to cling about my heart,
And never struggled to escape,
　And yet it did at last depart.

Oh happier far art thou than we,
　Who wander in the desert, blind, —
Thou hast left pain and poverty,
　And all the wrongs of life behind.

We strove whilst thou wast here (let's say
　Thus much to cheat our sorrow still)
To make thy life one sunny day,
　And shield thee, in our hearts, from ill.

During the next thirty years the life of Mr.
Procter was almost wholly uneventful. His appointment as Metropolitan Commissioner of Lunacy
was annually renewed, until he became one of the
permanent commission constituted by the Act of
1842. Up to this date his official duties were
limited to London, and the terms of his appointment allowed him to continue his private practice

as a conveyancer ; but from that year to 1861 the work of his office was more onerous, kept him constantly travelling about the country, and was legally, as well as practically, incompatible with the private exercise of his profession.

The earlier years of this portion of Mr. Procter's life were spent in a little Gothic cottage, opposite to the house of Sir Edwin Landseer, 5, Grove End Road, St. John's Wood.   After that, he and his family resided for many years at No. 13, Upper Harley Street — a house which will long be remembered with pleasure and regret by the many distinguished men and women who frequented its dinners and " at homes."   It was not till after he had resigned his commissionership, in 1861, that the family removed to 32, Weymouth Street, one of Mr. Procter's own houses.   Here, his and his wife's friendly receptions were for some years kept up, but on a more limited scale, for the Poet's health was not what it had been, and he was gradually less and less able to sustain his share in the pleasant burdens of hospitality.

The two great points of personal interest in Mr. Procter's later life were, first, the very distinguished position suddenly taken by his beloved daughter, Adelaide, as a poetess ; and, secondly,

5   G

her premature death, in 1864. Miss Procter, on
the publication of her " Legends and Lyrics," at
once assumed a high place in popular estimation ;
and that place she has maintained year after year,
and still maintains without any diminution, the
present demand for her poems being far in excess
of that for the writings of any living poet, except
Mr. Tennyson. An incident, which must have
been gratifying in the highest degree to the loving father, at the outset of his child's career as a
poetess, is thus related by Charles Dickens in the
memoir prefixed to the later editions of " Legends
and Lyrics : "

" Happening one day to dine with an old and
dear friend, distinguished in literature as ' Barry
Cornwall,' I took with me an early proof of the
Christmas Number of ' Household Words,' entitled, ' The Seven Poor Travellers,' and remarked,
as I laid it on the drawing-room table, that it contained a very pretty poem, written by a certain
Miss Berwick. Next day brought me a disclosure
that I had so spoken of the poem to the mother
of the writer, in the writer's presence ; that I had
no such correspondent in existence as Miss Berwick, and that the name had been assumed by
Barry Cornwall's daughter, Miss Adelaide Anne
Procter ! "

Mr. Procter had six children, four of whom are still living. Adelaide, and two of the other three daughters became Catholics — an incident which does not appear to have even ruffled the family peace and affection.

> That best portion of a good man's life,
> His little, nameless, unremember'd acts
> Of kindness and of love,

may almost be said to have made up the *whole* of Mr. Procter's life, during the later years of it. Even his official duties were so performed as to come into this category, and thereby they lost the repulsiveness that they must often have had for any equally sensitive but less kind nature. At one asylum a patient was described to him as incurably violent, continually tearing up her clothes, and the like. Something in Mr. Procter's manner and look must have greatly touched her, as he told her that he would give her half-a-crown, at his next visit, if he found she had been " good ; " for, when the following month with its visit came, she hastened to claim the faithfully earned reward, and was eager to show the clothes which she had *made* in the interval. His left hand did not know the good his right hand did. His friends could tell, if they chose, many such *secrets* as the following one, which the Editor has at first hand. A young man had just ended his morning call upon Mrs. Procter in Harley Street, and Mr. Procter, according to his kind custom, saw him downstairs, but not to the door. Begging him to come into his study, he said, "I hope you will pardon me for what I am going to say. I know your wife has been ill a long while, and the expenses of such a time must be heavy on you. Would this be of use to you?" offering a cheque for 50*l.*, and adding, "I shall not even tell my wife!" The young man had never hinted his need to Mr. Procter, or to any one else; nevertheless, this true friend had so well divined how his 50*l.* could be useful, that it was in fact the means of prolonging a beloved and inestimable life. This was *after* the date of a letter in which he writes, "I have been obliged to resign my Commissionership of Lunacy, not being able to bear the pain of travelling. By this, I lose about 900*l.* a year. I am therefore sufficiently poor, even for a poet." The 50*l.* were repaid; but the loan, like many other such made by the poet to his poorer friends, was made under circumstances which rendered it practically equivalent to a gift.

Mr. Procter continued to be an "Honorary

Member " of the Commission after he had resigned in 1861. His loss of income, through this resignation, was more considerable than it would have been, had substantial instead of technical justice prevailed in the fixing of the amount of his pension. This was calculated upon only twenty years' service, not upon the thirty he had actually served, because for the first ten, during which he had served as " Metropolitan Commissioner," it was *nominally* an impermanent appointment. Had he or his friends pushed his claims to have his retiring pension calculated on the whole period, it is difficult to suppose that they would not have been allowed, as such claims have been over and over again, in what appear to be exactly parallel cases. But he was not a man to make a fuss about his rights, or to allow others to do so for him.

A legacy of 6500*l.*, which had been left to him by his old friend, Mr. Kenyon, some two or three years before, made, indeed, the loss of 900*l.* a year less sensible to him than it would otherwise have been; and happily he was not, in his last years, obliged to alter in any perceptible degree the style of living to which he and his family had been accustomed.

In the latter days of the Poet's feebleness and sinking life, the friends who were most about him were the late Mr. John Forster and Mr. Robert Browning — to whom he had written, thirty-five years before —

> All good be thine! Thou'lt win a name of might,
> So thou wilt but obey thy Genius duly;
> Live; labor; do thy true soul's bidding truly,
> Through morn, and noon, and eve, and thoughtful night!
> Clear be thy dreams! thy lines like arrowy light!
> Pour out thy rich sweet numbers! Freely sing!
> Soar freely, like the eagle strong of wing!
> Or, if needs be, descend
> Amongst the poor and those who have no friend!
> Into their cellar-homes seek thou thy way,
> And lift their dark romances into day!

" It was Procter," writes Mr. Fields, " who, first in my hearing, twenty-five years ago, put such an estimate on the poetry of Robert Browning that I could not delay any longer to make acquaintance with his writings. I remember to have been startled at hearing the man who, in his day, had known so many poets, declare that Browning was the peer of any one who had written in this century, and that, on the whole, his genius had not been excelled in his (Procter's) time. ' Mind what I say,' insisted Procter; ' Browning will make an enduring name, and give another supremely great poet to England.'"

Mr. Procter had the faculty and generosity and courage to give full and immediate recognition to every new poet of real power. He pronounced, for example, his highly favorable verdict at once on the first appearance of Beddoes, whose brilliant letters to his brother poet are reprinted from his "Life," in the batch of correspondence at the end of this volume.

Mr. Procter had a learned love of painting, and was at one time the possessor of a valuable collection. This predilection and his love of music brought about him many great painters and composers. But he never was heard to talk as an *expert* upon these arts, or even upon his own; and the written criticisms upon poetry, in which he, from distant time to time, indulged, were rather expressions of a deep and right sympathy and admiration, than attempts to analyze or lay down the law. It has been made a matter of complaint by some of his friends that it was difficult or impossible to get him to reveal his opinions upon political, philosophical, and other matters, some of which lie at the root of life and action. Possibly upon some of these he had no opinions. Wisdom consists in the true direction of the will and intellect towards right objects, rather than in the precise definition of those objects. A man may see very well in which part of the sky the sun is, though its disc be hidden with haze ; and he walks by its light in a shady grove just as really, and possibly more steadily, than another who travels eying its outline through his smoked glass. Few men have surpassed Mr. Procter in the unpretentious and untalkative wisdom and fidelity of a right direction of heart and mind.

His friends will readily recognize Mr. Fields' sketch of his appearance and manner in later years : —

" The poet's figure was short and full, and his voice had a low, veiled tone habitually in it, which made it sometimes difficult to hear distinctly what he was saying. When he spoke in conversation, he liked to be very near his listener, and thus stand, as it were, on confidential ground with him. His turn of thought was apt to be cheerful among his friends, and he proceeded readily into a vein of wit and nimble expression. Verbal facility seemed natural to him, and his epithets, evidently unprepared, were always perfect. He disliked cant, and hard ways of judging character. He praised easily.

He impressed every one who came near him as a
born gentleman, chivalrous and generous in a high
degree."

Besides his occasional sketches and essays, most
of which were collected and republished in America, Mr. Procter wrote two prose works of a more
elaborate and serious character: the "Life of
Kean," published in 1835, and "Charles Lamb:
a Memoir," printed thirty-one years afterwards.
The poet's best friends must agree with the opinion expressed by Harriet Martineau upon the
"Life of Kean," that it "was a mistake. He
should not have been pressed to write it, and he
ought not to have yielded in a matter in which
neither his heart nor his taste could have been
interested. It afforded only too good a theme for
his critics of the 'Quarterly' to turn to account
when satirizing a Whig poet in 1835." Charles
Lamb's Life was quite another sort of theme, and
Mr. Procter, though then in the vale of years,
gave himself to it with a far different result.
The following letter, written to him by Mr. Carlyle, after reading this book, will make most
persons who are acquainted with it pleased to
find their own feelings expressed with such force
and brightness.

5*

"Dear Procter, — I have been reading your book on Charles Lamb, in the solitary silent regions whither I had fled for a few days of dialogue with Mother Earth and her elements; and I have found in your work something so touching, brave, serene, and pious, that I cannot but write you one brief word of recognition, — which I know you will receive with welcome; all the more as I especially *forbid* you to bother yourself with answering it.

"Brevity, perspicuity, graceful clearness; then also perfect veracity, gentleness, lovingness, justness, peaceable candor throughout, a fine kindly sincerity to all comers, with sharp enough insight too, quick recognition graphically rendered — all the qualities, in short, which such a book could have, I find visible in this, now dating, it appears, in your seventy-seventh year. Every page of it recalls the old Procter whom I used to talk with forty-two years ago, unaltered except as the finest wines and such like alter by ripening to the full; a man as if *transfigured* by his heavy laden years, and to whom the hoary head is as a crown. Upon all which another old man congratulates him; and says, with a pathetic kind of joy, his *Euge, euge.*

"No answer to this; I already forbade you.

Take it as an interjection; written merely for solace of my own poor heart. And so good be with you, dear old friend.

" With many kind remembrances to Mrs. Procter,
" I remain,
" Always yours faithfully,
" T. CARLYLE."

Among Mr. Procter's friends, in later life, no one seems to have won from him so much genial confidence and self-communication as Mr. James T. Fields, to whose charming papers on " Barry Cornwall and some of his Friends," in " Harper's New Monthly Magazine," the reader may be referred for more information about the Poet's ways and opinions than is to be found elsewhere.

The weariness and sometimes the despondency of age made their weight felt by Mr. Procter many years before the end. In 1857 he writes to Mr. Fields: " I shall never see Italy; I shall never see Paris. My future is before me — a very limited landscape, with scarcely one old friend left in it. I see a smallish room, with a bow-window looking south, a book-case full of books, three or four drawings, and a library chair and table (once the property of my old friend Kenyon — I am writing on the table now), and you have the greater part of the vision before you.   Is this the end of all things ?   I believe it is pretty much like most scenes in the fifth act, when the green (or black) curtain is about to drop and tell you that the play of 'Hamlet' or John Smith is over. But wait a little.   There will be another piece, in which John Smith the younger will figure, and quite eclipse his old, stupid, wrinkled, useless, time-slaughtered parent.   'The king is dead — long live the king!'"

The following passages are from the aged Poet's letters to Mr. Fields:

" Your De Quincey is a man of a good deal of reading, and has thought on divers and sundry matters ; but he is evidently so thoroughly well pleased with the Sieur Thomas De Quincey that his self-sufficiency spoils even his best works. Then some of his facts are, I hear, *quasi* facts only, not unfrequently.   He has his moments when he sleeps, and becomes oblivious of all but the aforesaid 'Thomas' who pervades both his sleeping and waking visions.   I, like all authors, am glad to have a little praise now and then (it is my hydromel), but it must be dispensed by others.

I do not think it decent to manufacture the sweet liquor myself."

" You must be good-natured and excuse me, for I have been ill — very frequently — and dispirited. A bodily complaint torments me, that has tormented me for the last two years. I no longer look at the world through a rose-colored glass. The prospect, I am sorry to say, is gray, grim, dull, barren, full of withered leaves, without flowers, or if there be any, all of them trampled down, soiled, discolored, and without fragrance. You see, what a bit of half-smoked glass I am looking through. At all events you must see how entirely I am disabled from returning, except in sober sentences, the lively and good-natured letters and other things which you have sent me from America. They were welcome, and I thank you for them now, in a few words, as you observe, but sincerely. I am somewhat brief even in my gratitude. Had I been in braver spirits, I might have spurred my poor Pegasus, and sent you some lines on the Alma, or the Inkerman — bloody battles, but exhibiting marks not to be mistaken of the old English heroism, which, after all is said about the enervating effects of luxury, is as grand and manifest as

in the ancient fights which English history talks of
so much. Even you, sternest of republicans, will,
I think, be proud of the indomitable courage of
Englishmen, and gladly refer to your old paternity.
I, at least, should be proud of Americans fighting
after the same fashion (and without 'doubt they
would fight thus), just as old people exult in the
brave conduct of their runaway sons. I cannot
read of these later battles without the tears coming
into my eyes. It is said by 'our correspondent' at
New York that the folks there rejoice in the losses
and disasters of the allies. This can never be the
case, surely? No one whose opinion is worth a rap
can rejoice at any success of the Czar, whose double
dealing and unscrupulous greediness must have rendered him an object of loathing to every well-think-
ing man. But what have I to do with politics, or
you? Our 'pleasant object and serene employ' are
books, books. Let us return to pacific thoughts."

" My wife's mother, Mrs. Basil Montagu, is very
ill, and we are apprehensive of a fatal result,
which, in truth, the mere fact of her age (eighty-
two or eighty-three) is enough to warrant. Ah,
this terrible *age!* The young people, I daresay,
think that we live too long. Yet how short it is to

look back on life! Why, I saw the house, the other day, where I used to play with a wooden sword when I was five years old! It cannot surely be eighty years ago! What has occurred since? Why, nothing that is worth putting down on paper. A few nonsense verses, a flogging or two (richly deserved), and a few white-bait dinners, and the whole is reckoned up. Let us begin again." [Here he makes some big letters in a school-boy hand, which have a very pathetic look on the page.]

" All our anxiety here at present is the Indian Mutiny. We ourselves have great cause for trouble. Our son (the only son I have, indeed) escaped from Delhi lately. He is now at Meerut. He and four or five other officers, four women, and a child escaped. The men were obliged to drop the women a fearful height from the walls of the fort, amidst showers of bullets. A round shot passed within a yard of my son, and one of the ladies had a bullet through her shoulder. They were seven days and seven nights in the jungle, without money or meat, scarcely any clothes, no shoes. They forded rivers, lay on the wet ground at night, lapped water from the puddles, and finally reached Meerut. The lady (the mother of the three other ladies) had not her wound dressed, or seen, indeed, for upwards of a week. Their feet were full of thorns. My son had nothing but a shirt, a pair of trousers, and a flannel waistcoat. How they contrived to *live* I don't know; I suppose from small gifts of rice, etc., from the natives."

" I shall never visit America, be assured, or the continent of Europe, or any distant region. I have reached nearly to the length of my tether. I have grown old, and apathetic, and stupid. All I care for in the way of personal enjoyment, is quiet, ease — to have nothing to do, nothing to think of. My only glance is backward. There is so little before me that I would rather not look that way."

" My youth? I wonder where it has gone. It has left me with gray hairs and rheumatism, and plenty of (too many other) infirmities. I stagger and stumble along, with almost seventy-six years on my head, upon failing limbs, which no longer enable me to walk half-a-mile. I see a great deal, all behind me (the past), but the prospect before

me is not cheerful.   Sometimes I wish that I had
tried harder for what is called Fame, but generally
(as now) I care very little about it.   After all —
unless one could be Shakespeare, which (clearly)
is not any easy matter — of what value is a little
puff of smoke from a review?   If we could settle
permanently who is to be the Homer or Shakespeare of our time, it might be worth something;
but we cannot."

" The most successful book of the season has
been Mrs. Browning's 'Aurora Leigh.'   I could
wish some things altered, I confess, but, as it is,
it is (a hundred times over) the finest poem ever
written by a woman.   We know little or nothing
of Sappho — nothing to induce comparison — and
all other wearers of petticoats must courtesy to
the ground."

" We read with painful attention the accounts
of your great quarrel in America.   We know
nothing beyond what we are told by the New
York papers, and these are the stories of *one* of
the combatants.   I am afraid that, however you
may mend the schism, you will never be so strong
again.   I hope, however, that something may

H

arise to terminate the bloodshed; for, after all, fighting is an unsatisfactory way of coming at the truth. If you were to stand up at once (and finally) against the slave-trade, your band of soldiers would have a more decided *principle* to fight for."

"Poetry in England is assuming a new character, and not a better character. It has a sort of pre-Raphaelite tendency which does not suit my aged feelings. I am for love, or the world well lost."

"I despair of the age that has forgotten to read Hazlitt."

During the last few years of the Poet's life, he and his friends were distressed by a great and growing indistinctness in his speech. For some time he seemed scarcely aware of the extent of this infirmity, and he would often put his clear and rapid thoughts into words, which were rapid indeed, but only intelligible to the most diligently attending ear. He withdrew more and more from social intercourse as he became more conscious of this disqualification for conversation, and his friends saw very little of him for a considerable time before the general failure of his health. His little journeys to the haunts of his infancy, in the hope of being able to discover the house where he had lived, and the school at which he had learned his alphabet, were among the chief occupations and pleasures of this time. To the old man, who had never lost the sweetness and simplicity of childhood, the love of these places came, like home-sickness. He did not succeed in finding the house or the school. Probably, in the lapse of eighty years, they had disappeared. At least, however, he could have his grave near where they had been : and this last hope was piously fulfilled by those to whom he had confided it.

These notes may be fitly followed by two testimonials : one from the Commissioner's official colleagues, the other " from England's youngest to her oldest singer." As the Poet's deepest delight was always in having faithfully discharged his nearest secular duty, let an " Extract from the Minutes of the Commissioners in Lunacy," dated 19th October, 1874, stand first.

" Resolved : —

" That this Board, having heard of the decease of their colleague, Mr. Procter, desire to express

their sincere and respectful sympathy in the loss
sustained by his widow.

" They also desire to express their sense of his
public services, as one of the Commissioners; and
their private admiration of his high character as a
scholar, a companion, and a gentleman.

" That this record be entered on the Minutes of
the Board, and a copy of it transmitted by the
chairman to Mrs. Procter."

The six Commissioners, as a further testimony of
their respect for their colleague's memory, presented
to Mrs. Procter a bust of her husband, by Foley.

The following lines by Mr. Swinburne, and those
by Mr. Landor with which this volume opens, are
obviously no merely complimentary eulogiums,
suggested by the partial admiration of intimate
friends.   Mr. Landor knew the subject of his
praise mainly by his poems, and Mr. Procter's
acquaintance with Mr. Swinburne was formed
when he was too old for that sort of relationship
to arise.   The splendid testimony of two such
poets and critics will make a reader who has any
modesty hesitate before he undertakes to fix the
place of " Barry Cornwall " among English poets
in a lower rank than they have indicated it to be.

MONDAY, OCTOBER 5TH, 1874.

(In memory of Barry Cornwall.)

In the garden of death, where the singers whose names are
    deathless
  One with another make music unheard of men,
Where the dead sweet roses fade not of lips long breathless,
    And the fair eyes shine that shall weep not or change
    again,
Who comes now crowned with the blossom of snow-white
    years ?
What music is this that the world of the dead men hears ?

Beloved of men, whose words on our lips were honey,
  Whose name in our ears and our fathers' ears was sweet,
Like summer gone forth of the land his songs made sunny,
    To the beautiful veiled bright world where the glad ghosts
    meet,
Child with father, and bridegroom with bride, and anguish
    with rest,
No soul shall pass of a singer than this more blest.

Blest for the years' sweet sake that were filled and brightened,
  As a forest with birds, with the flowers and the fruits of
    his song,
For the souls' sake blest that heard, and their cares were
    lightened,
    For the hearts' sake blest that have fostered his name so
    long,
By the living and dead lips blest that have loved his name,
And clothed with their praise, and crowned with their love
    for fame.

Ah, fragrant his fame as flowers that close not,
  That shrink not by day for heat or for cold by night,
As a thought in the heart shall increase when the heart's self
      knows not,
  Shall endure in our ears as a sound, in our eyes as a light;
Shall wax with the years that wane, and the seasons' chime,
As a white rose thornless that grows in the garden of time.

The same year calls, and one goes hence with another,
  And men sit sad that were glad for their sweet songs' sake;
The same year beckons, and younger with elder brother
  Takes mutely the cup from his hand that we all shall take.
They pass ere the leaves be past or the snows be come;
And the birds are loud, but the lips that outsang them dumb.

Time takes them home that we loved, fair names and famous,
  To the soft long sleep, to the broad sweet bosom of death:
But the flower of their souls he shall take not away to shame
      us,
  Nor the lips lack song for ever that now lack breath.
For with us shall the music and perfume that die not dwell,
Though the dead to our dead bid welcome, and we farewell.

A. C. SWINBURNE.

(Night of Oct. 14th.)

The grave of the poet is in the cemetery at
Finchley, and the monumental headstone has the
following inscription : —

BRYAN WALLER PROCTER

(BARRY CORNWALL),

BORN NOV. 21, 1787.   DIED OCT. 4, 1874.

———•———

HIS WIDOW AND CHILDREN HAVE GIVEN GLAD ASSENT TO THE
ERECTION OF THIS MONUMENT BY HIS OLD FRIEND,
JAMES WILKES, ESQ., KNOWING THE
GREAT LOVE HE BORE HIM.

PART II.

---◆---

RECOLLECTIONS

OF

MEN OF LETTERS, ETC.

PART II.

—————

THE following sketches are but a small portion of the portrait gallery which it seems to have been Mr. Procter's long-cherished intention to paint, and they are evidently nothing more than very rough draughts, the MS. having many double readings, notes to the effect of " correct this," etc. It is also to be remembered that they were not even commenced till the writer was long past the " three-score years and ten " which are the allotted fulness of man's age. In his preface to these memoranda the writer says, " In my seventy-ninth year I begin the task." It seems, however, that some of the notes must have been written before this time ; for a few paragraphs — especially of the account of the " London Magazine " and its staff — are repeated almost verbatim in " Charles Lamb : a Memoir," written in the poet's seventy-seventh year.

A passage of some length, consisting of a sort of

parallel between Lamb, Hazlitt, and Leigh Hunt, occurs in these memoranda and in the Memoir of Lamb. It is now given from the latter, as being probably the revised version. This passage, in ordinary course, would have been omitted here. It has been retained, because, of all Procter's friends, Lamb, Hazlitt, and Hunt seem to have influenced him the most; and it seems therefore proper that his views concerning them should be noted in this place.

"Charles Lamb, William Hazlitt, and Leigh Hunt formed a remarkable trio of men; each of whom was decidedly different from the other. Only one of these (Hunt) cared much for praise. Hazlitt's sole ambition was to sell his essays, which he rated scarcely beyond their marketable value; and Lamb saw too much of the manner in which praise and censure were at that time distributed to place any high value on immediate success. Of posterity neither of them thought. Leigh Hunt, from temperament, was more alive to pleasant influences (sunshine, freedom from work, rural walks, complimentary words) than the others. Hazlitt cared little for these things; a fierce argument, or a well contested game at rackets, was more to his taste; whilst Lamb's pleasures (except perhaps from his pipe) lay amongst the books of the old English writers. His soul delighted in communion with ancient generations; more especially with men who had been unjustly forgotten. Hazlitt's mind attached itself to abstract subjects; Lamb's was more practical, and embraced men. Hunt was somewhat indifferent to persons as well as to things, except in the cases of Shelley and Keats, and his own family. . . . Hazlitt (who was ordinarily very shy) was the best talker of the three. Lamb said the most pithy and brilliant things. Hunt displayed the most ingenuity. All three sympathized often with the same persons or the same books; and this, no doubt, cemented the intimacy that existed between them for so many years. Moreover, each of them understood the other, and placed just value on their objections when any difference of opinion (not infrequent) arose between them. Without being debaters, they were accomplished talkers. They did not argue for the sake of conquest, but to strip off the mists and perplexities which sometimes obscure truth. These men — who lived long ago — had a great share of my regard. They were all slandered; chiefly by men who knew little of them, and nothing of their good qualities; or by men 'who saw them only through the mist of political or religious animosity. Perhaps it was partly for this reason that they came nearer to my heart."

All the following sketches appear to have been written within a short time of each other, except that of Godwin, which is on different paper and in an earlier handwriting.

RECOLLECTIONS OF MEN OF LETTERS,

ETC.

I have been acquainted, more or less, with almost all the literary people of England who have flourished in my time. Few persons have known a greater number; partly from my having been an amateur only, having a great liking and respect for letters, and not having intermixed with politics.

Of the literary people whom I knew, some were noted for great and some only for moderate intellects; some for strong prejudices and passions; some for fine fancies, great ambition, tender hearts, clear visions, and other qualities or characteristics which served to make them remarkable in the world. Now, most of them are gone; almost all. They seem like so many waxen figures which were so clearly visible in former days, — which stood on this little stage so firmly, but have been swept off into the great outer darkness, or have melted away and been dissolved gradually by the consuming efflux of time.

I assure myself with some difficulty that of the many living figures, once so palpable before me, scarcely any now remain. It seems therefore almost a duty (at all events it is an occupation and an agreeable task) to place my recollections on record. Others have spoken with great ability of some of the writers of this age ; but I know of no one who stood out of the throng, and saw so many of them as I have seen. As a consequence, I must (if I complete my present project) recount some few things which have not been noted by other men. To throw myself upon the old excuse, I may add that I have been repeatedly urged to commit these my recollections to writing.

Accordingly (in my seventy-ninth year), I begin the task ; uncertain how far my memory will serve ; uncertain whether I shall live long enough to complete it ; and by no means certain of my ability to render it worthy of perusal.

I do not purpose writing my own biography. I have no pretensions to trouble the world with such a history. If I should speak of myself (as I must incidentally), it will not be in either a vain or querulous mood.   I do not assume (as I have already hinted) to have been other than a lover of letters, and a gazer and listener in the general scene. But the authors who were contemporary with my life have better claims to notice.

At one time I thought that to become an author, — *i.e.*, to write a book — was one of the most stupendous acts to be performed by man. My ideas on this subject have sustained an important change.   They have been improved by reflection ; by my knowledge of authors ; and by the perusal of many books that have been written. I have noticed, too, that the immortality inflicted by critics has sometimes speedily come to an end. A fame which has been pronounced eternal has been cut short by the caprices of the age. Poets and prosers who once wore very dazzling halos have been eclipsed ; and even the critic himself, whose decisions it was supposed were infallible and would extend to the latest posterity, is now amongst the men and things forgotten.   Even some of the best men, of whom it is now my intention to speak, are gradually descending into the deep obscure.   Wordsworth is no longer widely read ; Hazlitt's books have, as it were, subsided into a dead language ; and the racy humor of Charles Lamb lives chiefly in the remembrance of the oldest men. Has their style of writing, then, passed away ? Is it lost to all succeeding generations ? I do not know that we have acquired anything better. Is our writing clearer, more brilliant, or simply more daring, than it used to be ? It is perhaps harder, more unsparingly logical, more metallic. But does it exhibit richer veins of knowledge ? deeper thoughts ? finer fancies ? I can turn to some antique pages that look fresh even now. Perhaps one or two octogenarians might value them still ; and say — " We have not, after all, so far outstripped the old people, whom our sons and daughters despise."

What is older than knowledge ? In what year did the imagination begin to blossom ? When was humor first made known ? Plato is more than two thousand years old. Job is older, and Homer. Even Dante has reached his six hundred years ; and Shakespeare has claims (although he cannot contrive) to be obsolete.

Never let us forget the past, — the wise past, that has fed us, and taught us, and rendered us what we are. Rather, kneel down and thank the

6*   I

rich and faded centuries, that have left such jewels behind them.

On entering upon my narrative, I must premise that it will include others besides purely literary men; and that the space allotted to authors is not in proportion to their several merits, but is determined rather by my intimacy with each. The writers are not numerous who have pursued literature exclusively, as an occupation and means of livelihood. Thus Lord Macaulay was a member of the Council of India; Lord Jeffrey was a lawyer and a Lord of Session; Charles Lamb was a clerk in the India House; Sydney Smith was a parish clergyman; and so it has been with many men who have nevertheless distinguished themselves in letters.

I am not sure whether a profession, unaccompanied by hard labor, may not act as a relief from the strain and tension of the mind, which the composition of books alone (as the sole occupation of life, I mean) would assuredly produce.

REV. WILLIAM LISLE BOWLES.

Long before I mixed with literary men, I knew and saw a good deal of the Rev. Wm. Lisle Bowles, the poet. He was at that time rector of

Bremhill, in Wiltshire.   This was in the year
1805–1806.   I frequently went to see him at his
parsonage, and joined him (my flute with his
violoncello) in practising duets.   He knew much
more of music than I did, and appeared to be a
certain though not very rapid performer.   A
schoolfellow of mine, when at Harrow, had given
me Mr. Bowles' Sonnets, which I then greatly
admired; and I was therefore very ready, perhaps
not a little proud, to join the reverend poet in his
harmonious interludes.   As far as our acquaintance went, he was simply a player on the violoncello; for I never heard him speak of his sonnets,
or refer to poetry on any occasion.   When I saw
him again, after the lapse of many years, at
Mr Rogers' house in St. James's Place (1821
or 1822), he at once recognized me; and he
seemed pleased at my having obtained a little
popularity.

On this occasion, I remember that after breakfast he walked with Mr. Rogers and myself to
Lansdowne House, in Berkeley Square (to see the
pictures), he having the privilege of introducing
friends there.

Mr. Bowles had a blunt, almost a rough manner, which did not quite answer my preconceived

(immature) idea of a poet. I had imagined that I should see a melancholy man, pressed down by love disappointed, and solemn with internal trouble; I found a cheerful married man, with no symptom of weakness or sentiment about him. He had a pretty garden at his Bremhill parsonage, where he erected a hermitage,.and was unwise enough to endow it with a multitude of inscriptions; at which his neighbors were fond of laughing, as instances of affectation. For myself, I never saw anything affected or fantastic in this gentleman. His wife was a lady, tall, and of good manners; not ill adapted to a poet who had previously exhausted all his sorrows in song.

Mr. Bowles eventually became a prebendary of Salisbury, and died within the shadow of that lofty cathedral.

John Howard Payne. — Rev. George Croly. — Lord Byron.

It was in the year 1816 or 1817, I think, that I began to know men of letters generally. First, I was introduced to Mr. John Howard Payne, who had previously been upon the stage, and was known by the title of " The American Roscius." He was then about thirty years of age, very fair and fat, and had an exceedingly pleasant address. He was intimate with a few authors, and with many of the actors of the day ; these facts tended to raise our acquaintance into something like intimacy.   We used to meet frequently at each other's lodgings, or at the theatres, for which he readily obtained orders.   He had in hand a tragedy, on the old subject of Brutus (altered in part from an old play), which was eventually accepted at Drury Lane.   At this time, although tolerably well read in many of the old dramatists, I had never attempted any composition in verse.

By means of Howard Payne I became acquainted with Mr. Jerdan, editor of the " Literary Gazette," with the Rev. George Croly (afterwards Dr. Croly), with Mr. Young and Mr. Farren, the actors, and others.   I was subsequently a frequent visitor at the lodgings of Mr. Croly, in Frith Street, Soho, where he and his mother and sisters received company on one day in the week, and where some French and English and a good many Irish visitors used to assemble.   Mr. Croly was then theatrical critic for the " New Times," and he also wrote for " Blackwood's Magazine."   He had a large and not prepossessing person, and a dashing and somewhat imperious manner; held violent Tory opin-

ions; expressed them very energetically; and
played not unpleasantly on the violin. He was
author of a poem, in the Spenserian stanza,
entitled " Paris in 1815," which had a tolerable
circulation. Amongst the various gentlemen (Mr.
W. Curran, Mr. Wallace, etc.) who visited at Mr.
Croly's house, was a Mr. William Read, who had
published a poem, founded on an Irish legend,
called " The Hill of Caves." This gentleman
introduced myself and Mr. Croly to Mr. Leigh
Hunt, with whom I soon became intimate. Mr.
Croly, however, did not cultivate Mr. Hunt's
society.

The author of " Paris in 1815 " had great admirers amongst his Irish friends. His sisters —
who were naturally proud of his talent — were
persuaded, as they said, that George was destined
to " push Lord Byron from his throne." They
repeatedly asserted this, very frankly; but I never
heard that Lord Byron's equilibrium was at all
disturbed.

I had previously taken great interest in the fame
of Lord Byron (with whom I had been at school,
at Harrow), and I resented these prophecies,
which, however, need not have annoyed me, for
Lord Byron was incontestably a very powerful

writer, and in 1818 was the most popular poet of his day. I had not seen him since about 1800, when he was a scholar in Dr. Drury's house, with an iron cramp on one of his feet, with loose corduroy trousers plentifully relieved by ink, and with finger-nails bitten to the quick. He was then a rough, curly-headed boy, and apparently nothing more. In 1817 he had passed through various gradations of refinement; was a dandy, a handsome polished travelled man of the world, and was surmounted by a reputation outshining that of every cotemporary poet.

This is not the place to obtrude any opinion upon Lord Byron's poems, which indeed have already been more than sufficiently criticised.

I cannot, however, refrain from adding my small testimony to that of some of the former critics, by saying that, in my opinion, the poem of " Don Juan " could not have been written by any other author of the present century. The jests and turns which have been stigmatized as so many blots and sins of the author, are essentially portions of the poem, of its nature and character, and could not have been omitted or destroyed, except by radically damaging the poem itself.

In regard to Dr. Croly's poems, which were to

supersede those of Lord Byron, Hazlitt has said of
them (in his " Plain Speaker "), " A dull, pompous,
and obscure writer has been heard to exclaim,
' That dunce Wordsworth.' "

" This was an effusion of spleen and impatience,"
says Hazlitt, " that any one should prefer Wordsworth's descriptions to his (Croly's) *auctioneer*
poetry, about curtains and palls, and sceptres and
precious stones." On the name of the writer
being asked by Northcote, and the answer being
that it was " Croly, one of the Royal Society of
authors," Northcote replies, " I never heard of
him."

It was-in this manner that my knowledge of
literary men began. It was afterwards widely
extended. By Leigh Hunt I was introduced to
Keats, Peacock, Hazlitt, Coulson, Novello (the
composer of music), and to Charles Lamb. Hazlitt
took me to Haydon and Charles Lloyd; and at
Charles Lamb's evening parties I found Talfourd,
Manning, and the renowned Samuel Taylor Coleridge. Through Coleridge (or Lamb) I subsequently became acquainted with Wordsworth and
Southey; and I lived for a short time in a house
where Hartley Coleridge was sojourning. In 1819
or 1820, I visited at Mr. Rogers' house, in Saint

James's Place. There I met Campbell and Thomas Moore and Crabbe, Sir Walter Scott, and Mr. (afterwards Lord) Macaulay. I may perhaps speak of these in their turns. I mention them now, merely to explain through what channels my acquaintance with them (sometimes slight enough) commenced.

I knew some of these men intimately. The valet de chambre's apophthegm which tends to reduce all men, on close observation, from their natural heroic proportions to the minimum size, does not stand good in this case. I saw some of them tried severely enough, by poverty, by loss of friends, by opposition from the world, and other causes. Yet they went through all bravely, heroically. Some of them have, I think, been overpraised, whilst several have (I am sure) been grossly maligned.

WORDSWORTH. — SOUTHEY. — COLERIDGE.

The Lake Poets, as they are generally called (Wordsworth, Southey, and Coleridge), must be dealt with altogether. Although they differed materially in their tastes, their talents, and otherwise in the course of their journeys through life, they had nevertheless some elements in common.

They ultimately became Conservatives, one of them a Tory of high cast; but in the first instance their imaginations were awakened by the flames of the French Revolution, and at the beginning of their career they poured out their generous sentiments on the equality of mankind, on brotherly love, on universal justice, and the tyranny of kings.

I first knew Coleridge 'in 1819 (on the introduction of Charles Lamb) and Wordsworth and Southey not until 1822. Coleridge, very speculative, was full and running over with knowledge; Southey spoke like a man of business, curt and to the purpose; whilst Wordsworth was grave and solemn, limiting himself to one or two subjects of poetry or literature. Although ponderously eloquent, when stimulated, he was generally inferior to the others in ordinary talk. Nevertheless he was far away the greatest poet, and has influenced the genius and temper of his times beyond that of any other author. Coleridge — who of the three came nearest to him — put forth a comparatively slender portion of original poetry, and Southey's verse was entirely of a different order; it was as a denser vapor, floating in the ether below. Indeed, Mr. Southey was as much akin to an orator as to a poet; and his prose writing, clear and terse, was decidedly better than his poems, and better than that of his two friends.   Of this gentleman (Southey) I have little to say.   I was three or four times in his company; once at his house at Keswick, where I breakfasted and passed a few hours with him, and once at dinner, at the Rev. Mr. Cary's, where he spoke with extreme energy on political matters; singling out the demerits of some writers and reformers in a very pointed way. " Ay! they have sown the teeth," said he, " which will spring up some of these days in the shape of armed men."   This Cadmean hostility, bearing upon the friends of some of the party then present, in some measure disturbed the conviviality of the meeting.

Wordsworth was essentially a meditative writer ; drawing upon his recollections of the past rather than on the present for his themes.   He has been called a Pantheist, but this was surely an error. He looked indeed so constantly and intently on the outer world, that he saw its minute differences and inmost secrets, and these he elevated by his imagination and showed how they make their impress on the human mind, until they become akin to the mind itself.

" The sounding cataract
Haunted me like a passion," etc.

Wordsworth has dug out of nature the stones and moss and crumbling matters which common men tread upon, and contemplated them through his intellectual microscope, until they have yielded up all their beauty and meaning, and shown on what their motion and vitality depend. And all this knowledge he has kneaded and intermingled with such human matter as is allied to the earthy materials of his themes. The peasant, the beggar, the wagoner, the idiot and his mother, become the actors in his dramas, and we are moved by them and the common objects around them, instead of by those fierce internal throes and terrible disasters which make up the stature and grandeur of antique tragedy.

If Wordsworth's powers were generated by the French Revolution, they were nurtured and brought to maturity by solitude. He did not waste his youth in personal debates, or in quarrels about the rights and wrongs of persons; but in the loneliness of his life he had space and time for his thoughts. The rivers and hills and rocks were the nurses of his moods, and amongst his neighbor rustics he had not one to contest his opinions or to disturb them; so he grew up alone.

He was very poor. The injustice of Sir James Lowther, or of his representatives, deprived him of a considerable sum of money which was his due, but of which he had not the means to enforce payment. So he kept company with poverty, until his friend, Raisley Calvert, gave him the help which enabled him, as he says, "if frugal and severe," to follow his inclination and cultivate poetry as an art. How successfully this was done, is to be seen not so completely in his own verse as in the effect which his example and teaching produced in other writers. The rapid transition from stilted artificial phraseology to more truthful and simpler language, which occurred in the history of our poetical literature, was altogether owing to Wordsworth.

A most reliable friend of mine, who went to visit him at the period of his poverty, told me that he met him coming out of a wood where he had been laboriously gathering large quantities of nuts, and having a vast quantity of that fruit in a bag or apron before him; and this gathering was for the purpose of helping the·scanty meal to which his family had to sit down on that day.

Wordsworth's prototype was Milton, who was, of course, vaster and grander and more harmonious. Yet Wordsworth is occasionally very lofty when the subject allows or stimulates him to ascend. He is more real and more pathetic than his master, and resembles him in one respect, as being without any dramatic faculty.

As you read the verse of Wordsworth, his words frequently have a wonderful influence in assimilating your thoughts to his. You see the bare moors, round which the winds sweep — the hills over which the sheep move like a cloud — the sheaves, and sheets of snow — the poor cottager and the wandering pedlar — and all that comes to peasant life — its loves and hopes broken down by sickness and old age. The beggar chirps querulously; the shepherd toils wearily up the mountains. All that is cast upon the world by poverty comes forth, to live, and toil, and die. There are no crownings of kings; nor march of conquerors; no bevies of ladies or courtiers, who laugh and lie, who rise and flourish, and fall like the leaves in autumn; but common human nature pines and fades away, and leaves a sigh in the reader's breast, which it is long before he can forget.

Wordsworth was a tall and ungainly man ; with a grave and severe face, and a manner that indicated tranquillity and independence rather than high breeding. For many years previous to his death he dwelt at Rydal, in Westmoreland. His mode of life was favorable to the object that he had in view ; doing nothing but what it was a delight for him to do, and doing this only when he was disposed to labor. His " sole ambition and serene employ " was to write verses, to convince the world that his poems were better than all others ; and so " finally array his temples with the Muse's diadem." From all accounts that have , reached me, Wordsworth entertained small tenderness for persons beyond those who were nearest to him. In that innermost circle his affections were concentrated ; and there he dwelt supreme. After he lost his only daughter, his state of mind was very affecting. The neighboring cottagers used to tell how he would wander about, almost constantly on the hill-sides, very sad and lonely ; never holding any talk or communication (as theretofore had been his habit) with the peasants that crossed his path, but hoarding, and, as it were, enjoying that despair and sorrow which no one can ever feel except the parent for the dead child.

Just before his own death, having doubts as to the course of his illness, he made the inquiry of his wife, who said to him, " William, you are going to meet Dora."

Samuel Taylor Coleridge was like the Rhine,

> That exulting and abounding river.

He was full of words, full of thought; yielding both in an unfailing flow, that delighted many, and perplexed a few of his hearers. He was a man of prodigious miscellaneous reading, always ready to communicate all he knew. From Alpha to Omega, all was familiar to him. He was deep in Jacob Behmen. He was intimate with Thomas Aquinas and Quevedo; with Bacon and Kant, with " Peter Simple " and " Tom Cringle's Log ; " and with all the old divines of both England and France. The pages of all the infidels had passed under his eye and made their legitimate (and not more than their legitimate) impression. He went from flower to flower, throughout the whole garden of learning, like the butterfly or the bee, — most like the bee. He talked with everybody, about anything. He was so full of information that it was a relief to him to part with some portion of it to others. It was like laying down part of his burden.   He knew little or nothing of the art of painting; yet I have heard him discuss the merits and defects of a picture of the poorest class, as though it had sprung from the inspiration of Raffaelle. He would advert to certain parts, and surmise that it had been touched upon here and there; would pronounce upon its character and school, its *chiaroscuro*, the gradations, the handling, etc., when in fact it had no mark or merit or character about it.   It became transfigured, sublimated, by the speaker's imagination, which far excelled both the picture and its author.   Coleridge had a weighty head, dreaming gray eyes, full, sensual lips, and a look and manner which were entirely wanting in firmness and decision.   His motions also appeared weak and undecided, and his voice had nothing of the sharpness or ring of a resolute man.   When he spoke his words were thick and slow, and when he read poetry his utterance was altogether a chant.

One day, when dining with some lawyers, he had been more than usually eloquent and full of talk.   His perpetual interruptions were resented by one of the guests, who said to his neighbor, " I'll stop this fellow; " and thereupon addressed the master of the house with " G——, I've not

forgotten my promise to give you the extract from
'The Pandects.' It was the ninth chapter that
you were alluding to. It begins: 'Ac veteres
quidam philosophi.'" " Pardon me, sir," inter-
posed Coleridge, " there I think you are in error.
The ninth chapter begins in this way, 'Incident
sæpe causæ,' etc." It was in vain to refer to anything on the supposition that the poet was ignorant, for he really had some acquaintance with
every subject. I imagine that no man had ever
read so many books and at the same time had
digested so much.

Coleridge was prodigal of his words, which in
fact he could with difficulty suppress; but he
seldom talked of himself or of his affairs. He was
very speculative, very theological, very metaphysical, and not unfrequently threw in some little
pungent sentence, characteristic of the defects
of some of his acquaintance. In illustration of
his unfailing talk, I will give an account of one
of his days, when I was present. He had come
from Highgate to London, for the sole purpose of
consulting a friend about his son Hartley (" our
dear Hartley "), towards whom he expressed, and
I have no doubt felt, much anxiety. He arrived
about one or two o'clock, in the midst of a conver-

sation, which immediately began to interest him. He struck into the middle of the talk very soon, and held the " ear of the house " until dinner made its appearance about four o'clock. He then talked all through the dinner, all the afternoon, all the evening, with scarcely a single interruption. He expatiated on this subject and on that; he drew fine distinctions; he made subtle criticisms. He descended to anecdotes, historical, logical, rhetorical; he dealt with law, medicine, and divinity, until, at last, five minutes before eight o'clock, the servant came in and announced that the Highgate stage was at the corner of the street, and was waiting to convey Mr. Coleridge home. Coleridge immediately started up oblivious of all time, and said, in a hurried voice, " My dear Z——, I will come to you some other day, and talk to you about our dear Hartley." He had quite forgotten his son and everybody else, in the delight of having such an enraptured audience.

Coleridge lived at this time (1823) with Mr. and Mrs. Gillman, at the Grove, Highgate. They were most kind to him, and he repaid their tenderness with gratitude and sincere respect. Mr. Gillman was a surgeon; and his wife took a maternal or sisterly interest in Coleridge and his affairs.

S. ROGERS. — T. CAMPBELL. — THOS. MOORE.

I forget who introduced me to Mr. Rogers in
the year 1820.   He lived then and until his death
in Saint James's Place, in a house that had previously belonged to one of the Dukes of St. Alban's.
It was not in a wide street, but it looked south-
ward on to the Green Park.   Upon the whole I
never saw any residence so tastefully fitted up and
decorated.   Every thing was good of its kind, and
in good order.   There was no plethora; no appearance of display, no sign of superfluous wealth.
There were good pictures, good drawings, and a
few good books.   He had choice statuettes, some
coins, and vases, and some rare bijouterie.   There
was not too much of any thing, not even too much
welcome; yet no lack of it.   His breakfast-table
was perfect, in all respects; and the company —
where literature mixed with fashion and rank,
each having a fair proportion — was always agreeable.   And in the midst of all his hospitable glory
was the little old pleasant man, not yet infirm,
with his many anecdotes, and sub-acid words that
gave flavor and pungency to the general talk.
He dwelt too much (too much for the taste of some
of his hearers) on olden times, on the days of Fox

and Pitt and Sheridan, all of whom he knew and
mentioned with great respect, never omitting the
" Mr." previously to each name.   Like most other
persons he was, perhaps, too much disposed to
overvalue the times and people of his youth.
Even the authors of the last century, so manifestly
inferior to those of the present, found an advocate
with him.   He admired Gray prodigiously, and
had great respect for Mr. Crowe, the Professor of
Poetry at Oxford, whose " Lewesdon Hill " he
thought to be almost unequalled.   He had just
begun to admit Sir Walter Scott and Lord Byron
into his list of deservedly distinguished writers.
Crabbe he had always admitted amongst the great
authors, because of his style, and Mr. Thomas
Moore was rather a favorite by reason of his up-
holding the merits of Sheridan, whom he (Mr.
Rogers) had generously assisted in his later days.
He had no imagination, but give him the thing
imagined, and (if he liked it) he was tolerably sure
to suggest some improvement to it.   " Rogers'
rhymes " (which Lord Byron has praised) moved
on harmonious hinges ; but they on no occasion
had that free spontaneous sound which the lines
of the higher poets possess.   I like the versification
in his poem of " Jacqueline " the best.

It has been rumored that he was a sayer of bitter things. I know that he was a *giver* of good things — a kind and amiable patron, where a patron was wanted; never ostentatious or oppressive, and always a friend in need. He was ready with his counsel; ready with his money. I never put his generosity to the test, but I know enough to testify that it existed, and was often exercised in a delicate manner, and on the slightest hint. " I have received the kindest letter in the world from Rogers," said X—— one day, " inclosing a fifty pound note. God knows, it did not come before it was wanted." It appeared that a friend of mine had casually mentioned X——'s great distress, his struggles for bread, and his large family, a few days previously to Rogers, who made no observation beyond a little sympathy, but he took the opportunity of silently giving the money without parade.   .

He delighted in clever and pleasant anecdotes, and he told them well. Mr. Wordsworth was breakfasting with him one morning, he said; but he was much beyond the appointed time, and excused himself by stating that he and a friend had been to see Coleridge, who had detained them by one continuous flow of talk. " How was it you called so early upon him?" inquired Rogers. "Oh," replied Wordsworth, "we are gong to dine with him this evening, and —— " "And," said Rogers, taking up the sentence, "you wanted to take the sting out of him beforehand."

I met at Mr. Rogers' house Crabbe the poet, Mr. Wm. Spencer, Chantrey, Thomas Campbell the poet, and Sir Walter Scott, and in after years Mr. Macaulay. I never heard Rogers volunteer an opinion about Campbell, except after his death, when he had been to see the poet's statue. "It is the first time," said he, "that I have seen him stand straight for many years."

I have not much to recount in reference to Campbell, who, notwithstanding his precision and minuteness, has written some bold and magnificent songs, and whose "Hohenlinden" is charming. The proofs of his larger poems were, I believe, altered and blotted so mercilessly as to distract the printer. Nevertheless, there was a fund of impetuosity within him that, on sufficient provocation, burst through the rigidity of his general manner, and accounted for his sea and battle songs, which achieved such success. Campbell had small features, and wore a wig, which on one occasion he tore off, and said to Leigh Hunt, who had jested with him, " By gad, you villain, I'll throw my laurels at you." Hunt has, I think, stated this anecdote in his autobiography, or elsewhere.

Crabbe, when I first saw him, was an old gentleman, with white hair, and the mildest possible manner. He gave no indication of the vigor and shrewdness which he put forth in his verse. I remember that Moore was at Rogers' house one morning when Crabbe was breakfasting there, and when they were engaged to dine at some nobleman's house. Moore cautioned him, in the morning, to stand up and be manly. " For God's sake, Crabbe," said he, " don't be so *very* grateful when we go to Z——'s house to-night."

I come now to Mr. Thomas Moore himself, whose writings I confess I never greatly admired. They are very clever and polished, but to my taste terribly artificial. All that Burns had he wanted. I except a certain easy flow of words, the talent for producing which Moore had manifestly cultivated to the extreme point of art. He was a very little round-faced man, and had an easily worn but not unpleasant assurance. His estimates of persons seemed to depend much on their position or rank ; he did not trouble himself to discuss persons who had no rank at all.

In his diary or letters, published in Lord John Russell's memoir, he speaks of being present at two dinners, viz., at one where the company consisted of "some curious people" (I think that is the phrase), namely, Wordsworth, Lamb, Southey, etc., and at the other, where he met a "distinguished circle," consisting of Lord A., Lord B., Lord C., etc., all of whom are now duly forgotten. "Tommy loves a lord," as Lord Byron said of him. Moore's verses are for the most part overlabored, I think, and have a tendency to the epigrammatic, where simplicity would have better served. I was disappointed, on looking back at the Irish Melodies, lately, to find that there is scarcely one of first-rate excellence. Speaking for myself, I would rather have written three of Burns's songs than the whole collection. The vitality is preserved by the beautiful airs to which they are wedded.

His "Twopenny Post-bag," and other works of a similar class, are however very piquant and clever. The subjects accorded with his tastes. As to the songs and other poems one can seldom imagine that they were written in the open air, in the woods or fields, or in the face of nature. There is (so to speak) always a boudoir or indoor air about them: the very flowers seem to be arti-

7*

ficial. Mr. Moore's verses are also too saccharine:
they want substance and relief. One may be
smothered even with roses; and if the roses want
their natural dew and freshness, the suffocation
becomes unpleasant.

Sir Walter Scott.

Let us now turn to a different man. I first met
Sir Walter Scott at Mr. Rogers', at breakfast.
He was tall, stalwart, bluff but courteous, and
rather lame. I was at once struck with his bon-
homie and easy simplicity of manner. He talked
well and good naturedly, and was perfectly self-
possessed and very pleasant. Without the slightest appearance of pretension, he spoke like a man
well assured of his position. Statesmen, poets,
and philosophers of all kinds had sought his company, and he was admired by everyone, high and
low. I do not think that any one envied him more
than one envies kings. He was placed high beyond competition.

His ease and great general power impressed me
very strongly lately, when re-reading his Romances.
In his unaffectedness and the apparent uncon-
sciousness of strength he is unequalled. There
are no more spasmodic efforts in him than in

Fielding. In particular subjects, and on some
points, he is perhaps excelled by other writers.
Thus Mrs. Inchbald is more pathetic; Miss Austen
deals more effectively with ordinary domestic matters; and the narrative of Alexander Dumas carries one on more buoyantly than that of Scott.
The picture of Louis XI. in Notre Dame is surely
superior to the portrait of the same king in
" Quentin Durward," and Victor Hugo has originally more pathos and sometimes more force than
Sir Walter. But I see in no other author such a
combination of truth and ease and dramatic power.
What a fine easy natural out-of-door air his scenes
possess. What great geniality he has. What
picturesqueness, from the castle to the cottage,
from the religious zealot, and the soldier of fortune,
to the very hounds sniffing in the odor of supper
in " Redgauntlet." If he seldom or never pene-
trates into the innermost regions of men, how fresh
are all his outside sketches. He is always the
best with mere human beings. If he has a dwarf
or a superhuman character, he fails. But look at
the multitudes of men and women whom he brings
before you. There are Claverhouse and Balfour
and Bothwell, and the Baron of Bradwardine,
Dugald Dalgetty and Dinmont, and Dirk Hatter-

aick, Meg Merrilies, Rob Roy, and Jenny Deans and Rebecca the Jewess, and a hundred others. Look at the variety (and *distinctness* of character) in one book only, " Waverley ; " they are like bells " each under each." From Mac Ivor and Evan Dhu down to Callum Beg, from the Lord of Tully-Veolan and the Baillie to the wandering idiot boy, you never confuse or forget them.

Things come and go; people speak and act and pass away to other regions without any apparent effort. He does nothing visibly to retard them, or hurry them on to another scene. The events, by day and by night, flow on as they do on the common stream of time. Scott seems to have had no vanity. He never thrusts himself into the narrative; never forces in any other person or event, unduly. His tales are not wrought up to a great climax ; nor framed for a particular moral or purpose. He does not allow the early scenes to pass dully, and nerve himself up at last for one enormous effort. His books are an evidence of an able, well-balanced mind : there is nothing in excess.

I am always sorry when I see Sir Walter Scott weighed in the same scale with Shakespeare. They are not of the same class. One is the historian of certain events, the painter of habits and localities; the other proceeds from himself. The subject-matter of the one must be interwoven with past events, and depends upon them for its worth. The other is independent of all things; the emotions and figures which he creates have their origin in himself and nature alone. The one is temporal and the other eternal.

I never observed Sir Walter's self-possession disturbed, except on one occasion, when Rogers told him with a smile that Lady B——'s maid had hid herself amongst the male servants, on the landing at B—— house, to watch him as he went downstairs, the preceding evening. He seemed a little ashamed of his admirer. I met him (Scott) afterwards at breakfast, in Haydon's studio, when a circumstance occurred that threw a different light on his power of self-command. Charles Lamb and Hazlitt and various other people were there, and the conversation turned on the *vraisemblance* of certain dramatis personæ in a modern book. Sir Walter's opinion was asked. "Well!" replied he, "they are as true as the personages in 'Waverley' and 'Guy Mannering' are, I think." This was long before he had confessed that he was the author of the Scotch

Novels, and when much curiosity was alive on the subject. I looked very steadily into his face as he spoke, but it did not betray any consciousness or suppressed humor. His command of countenance was perfect.

EDWARD IRVING. — THOMAS CARLYLE.

In the year 1822 or 1823, Edward Irving came from Scotland to London, full of youth and energy, full of enthusiasm for his high calling. He had great eloquence, which he poured forth without stint. I knew him soon after he arrived; the most pure and hopeful spirit, surely, that Scotland ever produced.

If his manner had not been so unassuming, I might have felt humble before him. But he was so amiable and simple, that we all forgot that we stood in the presence of a giant in stature, with mental courage to do battle with any adversary, and who was always ready to enter into any conflict on behalf of his own peculiar faith. With one small defect, he was a very handsome man, well-proportioned, active, healthy; and not yet thirty years of age.

I never heard him utter a harsh or uncharitable word. I never heard from him a word or sentiment which a good man could have wished unsaid. His words were at once gentle and heroic. Having the most sincere friendship and admiration for him, I was once or twice tempted, in mixed company, to assert that he was more like one of the old apostles than anyone that had lived since. I was met by a shout of derision from a few of the readers and disciples of " John Bull," who happened to be present. Their opposition served to confirm my previous opinion.

I saw E. Irving once only in the pulpit; but I met him almost every evening in private familiar life, at a house * where I was very intimate. He had a great many Scotch traditions, and many interesting stories, principally of persons in humble life, which he told in a charming manner. I remember in particular his narrative of his being rescued from the· bed of the Solway, when the tide was coming in, which has been since published. I remember, also, how well he told the story of Carruthers and Johnstone, since printed by Mr. Carlyle, in " Fraser's Magazine." He loved to dwell on great and good men, and on noble actions. His memory could not apparently retain anything that was mean. His expressions, when

* Mr. Basil Montagu's.

not scriptural, were pastoral and homely. " I took my staff," he used to say, "and walked over the hills to X——." His ideas of happiness and comfort were all drawn from easy Scottish life; the class wherein he was born. Although he spoke with great energy of every bold or noble deed, his voice always deepened and softened with the pathos of the story, whatever it might be.

No one who knew him intimately could help loving him. No one who had any knowledge of his thoughts and mode of life could offer him any offence. Yet amongst strangers — ignorant of his high gifts, and sceptical of human worth — he was slandered and maltreated. One of the truest spirits breathing, his words were twisted from their purpose, and his sincerity discredited, by men as unworthy as unable to comprehend his character or value his truth.

Mr. Thomas Carlyle's epitaph upon him is one of the most touching things in all literature. I read it very often. One of the ablest men of our time, who knew him well, from youth to manhood; one not ordinarily profuse in panegyric; one whose opinions seem, indeed, to have been formed in a more chilling atmosphere, has recorded his love and reverence for Edward Irving. Carlyle's words come incontestably from the heart. He speaks of his short life (forty-two years only) — of his thorough truth — of his youth maturing in the Scotch solitudes — and, after abiding for a time in the cold northern city, of his being cast into this blazing Babylon, where he was at first smothered with caresses, and then denounced by the fickle veering idolaters who crawled at his feet. Yet not a fact could be urged against him, except that his opinions differed from theirs. So they cast him down into the satanic pit, amongst the refuse of their kind, and went on worshipping another image — some coarse Belial whom they had themselves manufactured, and transfigured into a god.

When Edward Irving was perplexed and excited by the fraud or madness that prevailed (" The Tongues," as it was called), he had been carried away from the wholesome communities in which he at first mingled, and entered that gross atmosphere of adulation that rose about him, — breaking down his fine intellect, — and finally weakening him until he died. Some who were nearest to him helped him on the wrong path, and his great modesty caused him to refrain from playing at once the scorner and unbeliever, and prevented

K

his absolutely denying the validity of appearances which were presented to him in a very deceptive light. Over-anxiety and over-labor had worn him down. The crevices in his celestial armor were then seen, and there the poisonous darts penetrated.

About this time — when the love of his admirers had departed, when the anger of his elders or magnates had been pronounced against him — a friend of his met him, walking wearily in the streets. The usual kind greetings passed between them. Irving said little beyond inquiring for some friends, who, as he knew, had loved him. His smile was as sweet as usual, but very sad, and his voice was feeble and had lost its old heartiness. When his friend returned home, he said, " I have met Edward Irving to-day: I think he is dying." And although he lived longer than was expected, he soon afterwards went back to his native Scotland, and died there.

It was said that neglect, or rather the cessation of general admiration, had killed him. This was not the case. He cared little for the incense which the rabble poured out before him so profusely. But it was to him a deep and abiding sorrow that men whom he thought to be his friends, — men in whom he had believed, and on whom he had lavished his affection,—should have stood out arrayed against him. What had he been doing, believing? Was the world, then, after all, a mere mirage? It seemed of little use to travel further. The delectable mountains had vanished. His work was over or of no value. After toil, to the weary traveller comes at least—rest. There was nothing left but to go back to the home of his youth, and die.

Edward Irving's life was very hopeful once: to some it was lovely; and his death threw a gloom upon many hearths. His last words are the words of a true believer:

In life and death I am the Lord's.*

Although Mr. Carlyle is still alive, yet, as he was such an intimate friend of Edw. Irving, and as I was, in fact, made known to him by Irving, I venture to place on record a short memoran-

---

* The verse of Joshua (xxiv. 15) appears to have been often in his mind. On my marriage, 1824, he gave my wife and me a large Bible; in the fly-leaf of which he expressed his kind wishes for our temporal and eternal happiness, adding:

"But as for me and my house,
We will serve the Lord."

dum in reference to Mr. Carlyle himself; whom, however, I have not seen for several years.

Mr. Thomas Carlyle, when he was introduced by Edw. Irving to Mr. ——'s family (of which I almost formed a part), in 1823, was fresh from Scotland. He was then already author of the "Life of Schiller;" and his strong German tendencies were already formed. He had grave features, a brown, florid complexion, and a simple, manly manner, not depending on cultivation so much as on the internal thoughts which gave it motion and character. I found him very sensible and pleasant; having some peculiar opinions, indeed, with which, it must be owned, I did not much disagree.

There can be no doubt that Mr. Carlyle is a very original thinker, quick, deep, and in many things differing from all other men. Whether he be right or not, in all cases, I do not pretend to offer any opinion. In general, the chance is in favor of the greater number; but not always, I suspect, in such themes as he has taken upon himself to discuss. He is a great master of pathos; and he impresses upon certain abstract words and phrases a weight of meaning that exceeds that of any other writer. Thus, when he speaks of

Manhood; of Labor; of Heroism; of Time; of Silence; and Eternity, there is a value and meaning that I have never seen elsewhere. The world (our home), and man, our likeness and our brother, are justly upheld by him as undeveloped miracles, about which we are apt to chatter and argue as on a common rule in arithmetic, but to which our boasted scientific discoveries are poor and trivial. He does not utter hymns in favor of prosperity: his advocacy is reserved for the humble, the slighted, and deceived, and for the poor who have no friends. This is generally his cause of defiance and support. In some remarkable instances, he has quite deserted this ground for others, which require explanation. I am afraid that he sometimes exhibits too much respect for mere power. Thus, although he speaks most tenderly of Edward Irving (his friend), most kindly of Charlotte Corday, of Burns, of Samuel Johnson, and others, against whom the thorns of the world pressed, his respect is also great for Danton and Robespierre, and he discovers admiration towards the old, cruel, crazy father of Frederick the Great.

Mr. Carlyle's style, which is at first repulsive, becomes in the end very attractive. His humor, although grave, is not saturnine: some of his

graver epigrams, indeed, pierce at once to the
very heart of a subject. He worships the hero ;
yet he is in general thoroughly radical. He loves
the poor worker in letters, the peasant, the
farmer with his horny hand, the plain speaker,
the bold speaker; yet he has no pity for the
negro, who, he says, should submit to slavery
because he is not fit for freedom. It follows from
this, that the man must remain poor who has not
obvious means to achieve riches, and that oppression and misfortune are reasonable decrees of fate,
against which our feelings should not cavil or
rebel. Mahomet the prophet, and Cromwell the
soldier, shine in his list of heroes ; and he loves
the real worker. He hates falsehood, and lazi-
ness, and puffery ; and he has little or no respect
for merely rich and titled people. The only
exceptions to this, his ordinary religion, are
Frederick surnamed the Great, and his father,
who was also great in the Tobacco Parliament,
but not elsewhere in the common world. This last
personage appears to me to sit on the very lowest
step of the seat of royalty ; very ignorant, very
obstinate, very mean, and unparalleled in Europe
as a troublesome family despot. The Memoirs of
Frederica Sophia Wilhelmina, Margravine of Bay-

reuth, afford some curious particulars of the pranks (exercitationes) of this crowned head. He cared for no man's opinion, good or bad. *Rex est qui nihil metuit.*

WILLIAM HAZLITT.

Justice has never been done, I think, to the great and varied talents of William Hazlitt. The opinion of the dominant party (" public opinion," as it is called) was directed against him during his life, and that opinion has continued to prevail, amongst the unthinking and easy multitude, ever since.

But public opinion is the opinion of the temporary majority. It is sometimes in favor of Whigs, sometimes of Tories, and is a heap of unexamined notions. It is continually swerving, from right to wrong. It is continually abandoning its own uncertain eminence. In times of Catholic and Protestant persecutions, public opinion was guided by its passions and prejudices (its weaknesses) alone. Sometimes it burned individuals of one sect, sometimes of the other. In matters of mere taste, perhaps, the sincere opinion of an independent, accomplished critic might be sufficient for his own and for future generations; but not otherwise.

Hazlitt himself had strong passions, and a few prejudices; and his free manifestation of these were adduced as an excuse for the slander and animosity with which he was perpetually assailed. He attacked others, indeed (a few only), and of these he expressed his dislike in terms sometimes too violent perhaps, and at no time to be mistaken. Yet, when an opportunity arose to require from him an unbiassed opinion, he was always just. He did not carry poisoned arrows into civil conflict.

Hazlitt held those extreme radical opinions which, fifty years since, were upheld by many others; and the warmth of his temper led him to denounce things and systems to which he had a strong aversion. Subject to the faults arising out of this his warm temperament, he possessed qualities worthy of affection and respect. He was a simple, unselfish man, void of all deception and pretence; and he had a clear, acute intellect, when not traversed by some temporary passion or confused by a strong prejudice. Almost all men come to the consideration of a subject (not mathematical) with some prejudice or predilection. And even a prejudice, as Burke says, has its kernel (which should be preserved) as well as its husk (which should be cast aside). Like many others, he was sometimes swayed by his affections. He loved the first Napoleon beyond the bounds of reason. He loved the worker better than the idler. He hated pretensions supported merely by rank or wealth or repute, or by the clamor of factions. And he felt love and hatred in an intense degree. But he was never dishonest. He never struck down the weak, nor trod on the prostrate. He was never treacherous, never tyrannical, never cruel.

The history of Hazlitt is like that of some of the scholars of former times, who were always face to face with misfortune. Merit (especially without prudence) is of insufficient strength to oppose injustice, which is always without pity. It seems to be a hopeless task to be always toiling up an ascent, where power and malignity united stand armed at the top. Then at one time he had ill-health, which added its weight to the constant obloquy with which he was assailed. To oppose this were the strength arising from a sense of injustice, and the native vigor of his own soul. He had a grand masculine intellect, which conquered details as well as entireties, and rejected nothing which helped the understanding.

8

The decisions of a hostile majority pressed down
(as I have said) the reputation of William Hazlitt,
and no one has taken the trouble to elevate it to
its proper position since. How seldom do we determine a question by our own reason! We adopt
the opinions of others, or we imperfectly discuss
the problem itself. What subject (except a mathematical proposition) has been unsparingly dis-
cussed; penetrated to its depths? Have moral
and religious questions ever been thoroughly
scrutinized? In newspapers and reviews I read
occasionally that the "essays" or "works" of Mr.
A—— or Mr. B—— are in their "third edition."
These books contain the dry and meagre thoughts
of individuals, couched in sterile language; well
advertised, indeed, and well puffed, — but which
elevate no one, which suggest nothing; whilst
Hazlitt's sterling sentences remain immured, to be
dug up, I hope, by some future explorer.

Hazlitt's range of thought was very extensive.
He wrote on books and men, on politics and manners. Metaphysics were not too remote from him,
nor was the stage too trivial or too near. In his
pages you may read of Berkeley and Hume, of
Jeremy Taylor and Sir Thomas Brown. You may
recreate yourself with Shakespeare and Milton;

with Wordsworth, with Pope, and Lord Byron.
He has commented on philosophers and divines, on
tragedy and comedy, on poetry and politics, on
morals, on manners, on style, on reasoning.

In astronomy and mechanics, in physiology, in
chemistry and general science, there have, I know,
been wonderful discoveries; but these, however
important, require in each case the possession of
only one particular talent, whilst Hazlitt's books
touch upon many subjects which lie beyond the
pale of science. To use his own words, " I have
at least glanced over a number of subjects —
painting, poetry, prose, plays, politics, parlia-
mentary speakers, metaphysical lore, books, men
and things." This list, although extensive, does
not designate all the subjects on which he wrote.

His talk (when not political) was principally on
books and on such anecdotes as brought out the
characters of individual men. In these last he
always allowed small facts and involuntary actions
to have their full share of weight. He himself
had no books, and he never borrowed them, except
for temporary reference. All his works were made
out of " the carver's brain." There was nothing
that he refused to discuss. Although encum-
bered by some prejudices (which he knew and

admitted), he would argue all subjects candidly.
In a Dialogue on Envy, between Northcote and
himself, Northcote is made to say — " Why do you
so constantly let your temper get the better of
your reason ? " To which Hazlitt replies — " Because I hate a hypocrite, a time-server and a slave ! "
This dialogue, it is to be remembered, was written
by Hazlitt *himself !* Northcote's accusation is not
denied ; but an excuse is offered for what the other
impliedly admits. Hazlitt must however not at all
times be held accountable for his arguments, for
some of them appear to be mere pieces of ingenuity ; as where he insists on the past being of equal
importance with the future, and on the disadvan-
tage of intellectual superiority.

Hazlitt's critical style, in all cases where he does
not overwhelm it by elaborate eulogy, is strong,
picturesque, and expressive. As a piece of eloquent writing, few passages in literature surpass
his " Introduction to the Literature of Elizabeth."
Leigh Hunt said, cleverly, that his " criticisms on
art threw a light on the subject as from a painted
window."

He had a very quick perception of the beauties
and defects of books. When he was about to
write his " Lectures on the Age of Elizabeth," he

knew little or nothing of the dramatists of that time, with the exception of Shakespeare. He spoke to Charles Lamb, and to myself, who were supposed by many to be well acquainted with those ancient writers. I lent him about a dozen volumes, comprehending the finest of the old plays; and he then went down to Winterslow Hut, in Wiltshire, and after a stay of six weeks came back to London, fully impregnated with the subject, with his thoughts fully made up upon it, and with all his lectures written. And he then appeared to comprehend the character and merits of the old writers more thoroughly than any other person, although he had so lately entered upon the subject.

No man was competent to write upon Hazlitt who did not know him personally. Some things of which he has been accused were referable merely to temporary humor or irritability, which was not frequent, and which was laid aside in an hour. At other times (by far the greater portion of his life) he was a candid and reasonable man. He felt the injuries and slanders, however, which were spit forth upon him, acutely; and resented them. He was not one of those easy, comfortable, and so-called "good-natured" men, who are simply inaccessible to strong emotions, and from whom the minor ills of life fall off, without disturbing them, like rain from a pent-house top.

His essays are full of thought; full of delicate perceptions. They do not speak of matters which he has merely seen or remembered, but enter into the rights and wrongs of persons; into the meaning and logic of things; into causes and results; into motives and indications of character. He is, in short, not a *raconteur* but a reasoner. This will be observed in almost all his numerous essays. If he is often ostentatious, that is to say, if he accumulates image upon image, reason upon reason, it is simply that he is more in earnest than other writers.

In addition to these general qualities, how felicitous are many of his obiter remarks! They deserve to be enshrined by some abler workman than myself.

In his criticism on "Antony and Cleopatra," what can be truly finer than his oriental conclusion: "Shakespeare's genius has spread over the whole play a richness like the overflowing of the Nile."

Of George Dyer, who passed his life amongst old books, without entering into the spirit of the authors, he says — "He hangs like a film and cobweb upon letters, or like the dust on the outside of knowledge, which should not too rudely be brushed aside."

Of Charles Lamb he says — " He always made the best pun and the best remark in the course of the evening.   No one ever stammered out such fine, piquant, deep, eloquent things in half-a-dozen sentences as he does.   His jests scald like tears, and he probes a question with a play upon words."

Of Lord Byron he says — " He towers above his fellows by all the height of the peerage."

" Leigh Hunt," he says, " has a fine vinous spirit about him, and tropical blood in his veins. But he requires a select circle of admirers to feel himself quite at home.   His hits do not tell like Lamb's : you cannot repeat them the next day."

" Modesty is the lowest of the virtues, and is a real confession of the deficiency which it indicates. He who undervalues himself is justly undervalued by others."

" If you marry, marry the woman you like. Nothing will atone for, or overcome an original distaste."

" A spider, my dear, the meanest thing that crawls or lives, has its mate or fellow; but a scholar has no mate or fellow."

" Our universities have become, in a great measure, cisterns to hold, not conduits to disperse, knowledge.   The age has the start of them."

These few are picked up carelessly; but there are hundreds of others.

My first meeting with Mr. Hazlitt took place at the house of Leigh Hunt, where I met him at supper. I expected to see a severe, defiant-looking being. I met a grave man, diffident, almost awkward in manner, whose appearance did not impress me with much respect. He had a quick, restless eye, however, which opened eagerly when any good or bright observation was made; and I found at the conclusion of the evening, that when any question arose, the most sensible reply always came from him. Although the process was not too obvious, he always seemed to have reasoned with himself before he uttered a sentence. And the reader of his essays will recollect that the same process is observable there. There is less of what he sees or hears or remembers, than what seems to arise from some logical or internal movement. Sometimes, indeed, he carries his habit of reasoning too far — and hence arises something that excites a doubt; but this may be called the *excess* of truth.

I saw a great deal of Hazlitt during the last twelve or thirteen years of his stormy, anxious, uncomfortable life. And in offering my estimate

of him, I need only adopt the words of his de-
fender, Charles Lamb, viz. : — " Protesting against
things that he has written, and some things which
he chooses to do, I should belie my conscience if I
said less than that I think W. H——, in his natural and healthy state, one of the finest and wisest
spirits breathing."   In 1819 he resided in a small
house in York Street, Westminster, where I visited
him, and where Milton had formerly dwelt; afterwards he moved from lodging to lodging, and
finally went to live at No. 6, Frith Street, Soho,
where he fell ill and died.   I went to visit him
very often during his late *breakfasts* (when he
drank tea of an astounding strength), not unfrequently also at the Fives Court, and at other
persons' houses ; and once I dined with him.   This
(an unparalleled occurrence) was in York Street,
when some friend had sent him a couple of Dork-
ing fowls, of which he suddenly invited me to
partake.   I went, expecting the usual sort of
dinner ; but it was limited solely to the fowls and
bread.   He drank nothing but water, and there
was nothing but water to drink.   He offered to
send for some porter for me, but being out of
health at the time, I declined, and escaped soon

8*   L

after dinner to a coffee-house, where I strengthened myself with a few glasses of wine.

Do I mention this spare entertainment as a charge against Hazlitt? Oh no, I do not; on the contrary, I was sure that the matter had never entered into his mind. He drank water only, and lived plainly, and not unreasonably assumed that what sufficed for himself was sufficient for others. He had nothing that was parsimonious or mean in his character, and I believe that he never thought of eating or drinking, except when hunger or thirst reminded him of these wants. With the exception of a very rare dinner or supper with a friend or intimate, his time was generally spent alone. After a late breakfast he took his quire of foolscap paper, and commenced writing (in a large hand almost as large as text) his day's work. I never saw any rough draft or copy. He wrote readily — not very swiftly, perhaps, but easily, as if he had made up his mind — the manuscript that I believe went to the printer. In his latter years he dined generally at the Southampton Coffee-house, in Southampton Buildings, and was much interested by the sayings of people whom he met there; and would often repeat and comment on them when they served to develop character.

Hazlitt was of the middle size, with eager, expressive eyes ; near which his black hair, sprinkled sparely with gray, curled round in a wiry, resolute manner. His gray eyes, not remarkable in color, expanded into great expression when occasion demanded it. Being very shy, however, they often evaded your steadfast look. They never (as has been asserted by some one) had a sinister expression ; but they sometimes flamed with indignant glances, when their owner was moved to anger ; like the eyes of other angry men. At home, his style of dress (or undress) was perhaps slovenly, because there was no one to please ; but he always presented a very clean and neat appearance when he went abroad. His mode of walking was loose, weak and unsteady ; although his arms displayed strength, which he used to put forth when he played at rackets with Martin Burney and others. He played in the old Fives Court (now pulled down) in St. Martin's Street; and occasionally exhibited impatience when the game went against him. It was here that he witnessed the play at fives of the celebrated John Cavanagh, of whom he has written so delightfully.

He lived mainly alone — the life of a solitary thinker. This gave originality to some of his essays; sometimes it deprived him of the advantage of comparing his opinions with those of others.

There is no doubt that his strong passions and determined likings often interfered with his better reason. His admiration of Napoleon would not allow of any qualification. And in the case of the heroine of the Liber Amoris (Sarah Walker), his intellect was completely subdued by an insane passion. He was, for a time, unable to think or talk of anything else. He abandoned criticism and books as idle matters; and fatigued every person whom he met by expressions of his love, of her deceit, and of his own vehement disappointment. This was when he lived in Southampton Buildings, Holborn. Upon one occasion I know that he told the story of his attachment to five different persons in the same day, and at each time entered into minute details of his love story. "I am a cursed fool," said he to me. "I saw J—— going into Wills' Coffee-house yesterday morning; he spoke to me. I followed him into the house; and whilst he lunched I told him the whole story. Then" (said he) "I wandered into the Regent's Park, where I met one of M——'s sons. I walked

with him some time, and on his using some
civil expression, by God! sir, I told him the whole
story." [Here he mentioned another instance,
which I forget.] "Well, sir" (he went on),
"I then went and called on Haydon; but he
was out. There was only his man, Salmon, there;
but, by God! I could not help myself. It all
came out; the whole cursed story! Afterwards
I went to look at some lodgings at Pimlico.
The landlady at one place, after some explana-
tions as to rent, etc., said to me very kindly, 'I
am afraid you are not well, sir?'—'No, ma'am,'
said I, 'I am not well;' and on inquiring further,
the devil take me if I did not let out the whole
story, from beginning to end!"

I used to see this girl (S. W.) at his lodgings in
Southampton Buildings, and could not account
for the extravagant passion of her admirer. She
was the daughter of the lodging-house keeper.
Her face was round and small, and her eyes were
motionless, glassy, and without any speculation
(apparently) in them. Her movements in walking
were very remarkable, for I never observed her
to make a step. She went onwards in a sort of
wavy, sinuous manner, like the movement of a
snake. She was silent, or uttered monosyllables

only, and was very demure. Her steady, unmoving gaze upon the person whom she was addressing was exceedingly unpleasant. The Germans would have extracted a romance from her, endowing her perhaps with some diabolic attribute.

To this girl he gave all his valuable time, all his wealthy thoughts, and all the loving frenzy of his heart. For a time, I think, that on this point he was substantially insane ; certainly beyond self-control. To him she was a being full of witchery, full of grace, with all the capacity of tenderness. The retiring coquetry, which had also brought others to her, invested her in his sight with the attractions of a divinity, — of a divinity, indeed, like those of old, when the goddesses lowered themselves for a while only to the entreaties of mortals, but reserved their permanent affection for the gods themselves.

BEDDOES.

Thomas Lovell Beddoes — claiming a literary ancestry from both father and mother (who was an Edgeworth) — was a writer of very early promise, and was afterwards the author of a drama, "Death's Jest Book," which has great power, and, in many respects, first-rate excellence. It shows how inadequately fame is awarded, when his merits have been so sparingly recognized (scarcely known indeed) up to the present time. He came before the public just when Wordsworth had overcome neglect and had grown into popularity, and soon after the genius of Keats and Shelley (after much perverse dissent) began to make way into the admiration of all persons having any claim to be considered as acute critics.

Beddoes in person and otherwise was not unlike Keats. Both were short in stature, and independent in manner, and very brief and decided in conversation. Beddoes was too fond of objecting and carping, when the merits of any modern books came into discussion. Not that he was at all vain or envious himself, but he was at all times unwilling to yield homage to any poets, except Shelley and Keats and Wordsworth. Of these Shelley was undoubtedly his favorite. Like that great poet, Beddoes had much love for philosophical questions, although the poetical element was predominant in him.

A very interesting memoir of Beddoes was — after his death, in January, 1849 — published by Mr. Kelsall; and I prefer referring to this memoir for particulars respecting the poet, for I could only

repeat them in this place. T. L. Beddoes was
educated at the Charter House, from which place
he went to Pembroke College, Oxford, where he
took his Master's degree. Subsequently he studied
medicine and surgery at Gottingen and other
places in Germany — Wurzburg, Zurich, Frank-
fort, and finally died at Basle, from a wound
received whilst dissecting ; his death being accel-
erated by a fall from his horse, by which his leg
suffered a terrible compound fracture.

" He wakes or sleeps with the enduring dead." — *Adonais.*

HAYDON.

Benjamin Robert Haydon — who lived under
the ban of the Royal Academy — was a careless,
boisterous, confident, pugnacious man. He was
always an enthusiastic artist, and at one time an
artist full of promise. When he exhibited his first
picture, many persons (not altogether ignorant of
art) thought it likely that he might become the
first English painter of his time. But his tendency
was to dash and hurry and exaggerate ; and his
pictures in their details did not answer all that his
friends had prophesied. In some of them, indeed,
there are portions which few of his cotemporaries
have surpassed. In the Judgment of Solomon, for

instance, some of the secondary figures seem scarcely inferior to Rubens.

Haydon had the look of a decided man: in painting, he certainly had acquired and pronounced very unequivocal opinions. His look and motion were assured; his sentences were without qualification; and his voice — which ordinarily was simply firm — in cases of earnestness or merriment was explosive. He appeared to be fonder of pronouncing an opinion than of pondering over it. His prominent delusion was that paintings, in order to become great as works of art, must be necessarily large in size; and this delusion he for some time acted upon as an established truth. The consequence was that his pictures were sometimes coarsely painted, and that he was obliged to neglect those particular excellences which are the results of care and which frequently attract purchasers. He was a vigorous draughtsman, and constant in carrying into effect his own theory; but he failed in stamping upon his figures individual character, for which the great painters have been celebrated.

He was a lecturer as well as a painter, and his earnest utterance must have impressed upon his hearer a conviction of his sincerity. I was informed (for I did not hear them) that the lectures were very able. Very picturesque and energetic they were, I am sure, for his conversation always was so. In describing any striking scene or hurried event he was unrivalled. He dashed off a vigorous narrative, without stopping to punctuate or qualify, and without descending to minute or unimpressive particulars. His description of rain was like a thunder-shower; and of an extensive landscape, a space without end. When he spoke, his very earnest manner gave his hearers the notion that he was always uttering and anxious for the truth.

Haydon was as resolute as pugnacious. He quarrelled with the Royal Academy, who did not do themselves much honor in altogether ignoring him. By gentle means on their part, — by submitting to friendly counsel, perhaps, on his own, — Haydon probably might have grown up to the stature of a great artist. Most of his chalk sketches were distinguished by fine and free drawing; but he was generally striving for something beyond his might — he was generally on the strain; was at issue with the successful members of his profession; always endeavoring to paint larger and grander pictures than other men; aiming not so much at positive good as at comparative excellence. Then his limited means forced him to exhibit for money, and afterwards to sell, pictures to which he had not been able to give that time and thought, which otherwise might have ensured success and obtained for him a distinguished name.

Haydon was almost always in poverty, and his uneasy life was ended by his own hand. The memoir and autobiography which appeared soon after his death was commented on without mercy. His suicide and groundless ambition were denounced as faults, or sins beyond the bounds of charity or forgiveness. . Yet, after all, his was surely a pitiable story. He was at one time taught to believe himself a great painter. His friends assured him that he was so, and the success of his early works convinced him that this was true. He was sanguine beyond all other artists; beyond most other men. He had much talent, of which he was very conscious; violent passions; proud irrepressible hopes; delusions, if you will, on this head in an unreasonable degree. The very extent and character of these carried him beyond the limits of common sufferers. It is not enough to argue that a man's own ambition has no solid foundation in other minds.   There it was, in the mind on which it was destined to operate.

The ground on which the poor painter stood (or seemed to stand, it is all the same) was cut from under him ; his hopes were swept away as worthless dreams ; the value of all that he had done was denied ; the study and energy of his life was derided ; even the very meal for to-morrow was to be torn away.   What could be the end of all this but —death ?   That would satisfy his creditors ; that would check, perhaps, his enemies ; that would allay the anguish in his heart.   In cases of death we generally volunteer a little pity : oftentimes we offer some excuses for the person dead.   Let us do so in this case.

Thomas Griffiths Wainwright.

. . . Who would have supposed that from a man who was absolutely a fop, finikin in dress, with mincing steps, and tremulous words, with his hair curled and full of unguents, and his cheeks painted like those of a frivolous demirep, would flame out ultimately the depravity of a poisoner and a murderer? . . .

Thomas Griffiths Wainwright became a contributor to the " London Magazine " at its first appearance. He at that time lived in handsome lodgings in Great Marlborough Street, which had theretofore been occupied by Mrs. Siddons ; and he appeared to be in possession of a competent income. Mr. John Scott, who had been previously acquainted with him, accepted his clever but very fantastic essays as a relief from the more serious papers of his other friends. These essays are upon works of art : they exhibit much cleverness and great affectation. To persons not acquainted with his manner, it may be sufficient to say that he never adverted to any painter by his usual name, but spoke of Julio Romano as Julio Pippi, of Paul Veronese as Cagliari, and of Titian as Vecelli. Wainwright was the nephew of Mr. Griffiths, for many years editor and proprietor of the " European Review." According to the stories current, he had originally been in some regiment of the line, and in the course of his early years had spent a couple of fortunes. He and his wife (once a Miss Abercrombie) began, it was said, at once on the principal money, and did not leave off until they came to the end. On the death of Mr. Griffiths, Wainwright came into possession of more property, part of it consisting of an excellent house and large grounds at Turnham Green. On one

occasion Mr. Richard Westall (the Royal Acade-
mician) and I dined there ; Wainwright's wife, her
son (a little boy), and her sister, Marian Abercrombie, a fair, innocent-looking girl, about nineteen years old, being present. Although I had
known Wainwright for two or three previous
years, I was not aware till then that he had a
child. Indeed, he seemed to have little affection
for the boy, who (scandal whispered) was the son
of a dissipated and impoverished peer. Mrs. Wainwright was a sharp-eyed, self-possessed woman,
dressing in showy, flimsy finery. She seemed to
obey Wainwright's humors and to assist his needs ;
but much affection did not apparently exist between
them.

Wainwright's conversation ran principally on
matters connected with art. He spoke especially
of German art, which he admired, and of German
literature, which had then (about 1826) scarcely
begun to make way in England. Mr. Westall and
I found that he had recently contracted intimacies
with some German art-students, and that he had
been buying and dealing with scarce old prints
and etchings to a great extent. Amongst these
were some very costly engravings after Marc
Antonio and Bonasone, which he had purchased

from Mr. Dominic Colnaghi upon trust, and parted with by mortgage or sale immediately afterwards. Subsequently he purchased very cheap copies of the *same* prints, and placed these on the card-boards, which had large prices noted on them in Mr. Colnaghi's writing, and from which the expensive specimens had been removed. These he sold for various sums far exceeding their value. Collectors know that a very fine impression of a rare old print has sometimes fetched 100*l.* or more, whilst a bad retouched copy may be bought for half-a-crown or a shilling. Besides this mode of obtaining money for his pleasures, W. had recourse to loans. Amongst others, he applied to me for a loan of 200*l.*, which it was not convenient to me, at that time, to advance.

Finally, having by means of forgery obtained a large sum of Stock, it became necessary for him to leave England. He accordingly absconded to France, and resided for some time at Calais and also at Paris. In the former place he became personally intimate with a married female, whom fear of detection or some other strong motive induced him to poison. Not only was this female fond of him, but her sister also became attached to him, and subsequently followed him to England, when he returned there.   During his residence in Paris he fell into extreme destitution.   At this time I received a letter from him, asking for a very small loan or gift in money, which I of course sent to him.   The letter was in his usual fantastic style, referring to some pictures which I then had, particularly to my " dusk Giorgione," as he termed it. But when he had to tell of his wretched state, his tone deepened.   " Sir, I starve," he said, adding that he had been obliged to pawn his only shirt, in order to enable him to pay the postage of the letter. His letter exhibited great depression.   He spoke of the crowds of gay and careless people — gamblers and prodigals and others, all of whom passed him by — whilst he was without a meal, without a single acquaintance, and not knowing where he could apply with the smallest chance for help.   From Paris and Calais he sent over dismal letters to various persons in England for a little help.   I pleaded for him to one or two of his acquaintance, without (I am afraid) much effect.

He must have had strong motives for communicating with England, when he was induced (notwithstanding his liability to arrest) to venture to London.   Here he was discovered almost immediately on his arrival.   He was talking to a female, near a lamp, in Howland Street, Fitzroy Square, when he was seen by a policeman, who knew his person, and captured him. "Mr. Wainwright," the policeman said, "I have been looking after you for a considerable time." The forgery of which he had been guilty brought him to trial, and notwithstanding his several murders, he was, by some curious arrangement (the legality of which I never comprehended), ultimately tried for forgery only and sentenced to transportation for life. His manner and accomplishments (such as they were) rescued him from the condition of a common poisoner, and lifted him into professional life. He acquired, in fact, some reputation as an artist, and painted portraits with some success. Here his history ended; for after a painful illness, in which he altogether lost the control of his mind, he died, raving mad.

In person, Wainwright was short and rather fat, with a fidgety, nervous manner, and sparkling twinkling eyes, that did not readily disclose their meaning. These, however, had no positive hardness or cruelty. His voice was like a whisper, wanting in firmness and distinctness. A spectator would, at first sight, have pronounced him thoroughly effeminate, had not his thick and sensual lips counterbalanced the other features, and announced that something of a different nature might disclose itself hereafter. His private selection of books, although small, was curious. It showed that he liked writers on astrology and the occult sciences ; and I remember particularly that he had two or three old books on poisons. These were richly bound (by Roger Payne), and must have been sold at his sale, unless he parted with them at his mother-in-law's death.

This was the man (deficient in the common elements of a murderer) by whom his wife's mother and sister, his own uncle, and the married lady at Calais, were without doubt poisoned. He was not entirely cruel. I imagine that he was perfectly indifferent to human life, and that he sacrificed his victims without any emotion, and for the purpose simply of obtaining money to gratify his luxury. Sometimes I have suspected him of gambling. . . . He was like one of those creatures, seemingly smooth and innocuous, whose natural secretions, when once excited, become fatal to those against whom they are accidentally directed.

LEIGH HUNT AND KEATS.

When I first visited Leigh Hunt (1817), he lived at No. 8, York Buildings, in the New Road. His house was small, and scantily furnished. In it was a tiny room, built out at the back of the drawing-room or first floor, which he appropriated as a study, and over the door of this was a line from the "Faery Queen" of Spenser, painted in gold letters. On a small table in this study, covered with humble green baize, Leigh Hunt sat and wrote his articles for the "Examiner" and "Indicator," and his verses. He had very few books, an edition of the Italian Poets in many volumes, Spenser's works, and the minor poems of Milton (edited by Warton) being, however, amongst them. I don't think that there was a Shakespeare. There were always a few cut flowers, in a glass of water, on the table.

Hunt was a little above the middle size, thin and lithe. His countenance was very genial and pleasant. His hair was black; his eyes were very dark, but he was short-sighted, and therefore perhaps it was that they had nothing of that fierce glance which black eyes so frequently possess. His mouth was expressive, but protruding;

as is sometimes seen in half-caste Americans. It was shortly after my first visit that I first met Charles Lamb, Hazlitt, Peacock, Walter Coulson, and others at supper there. Hunt never gave dinners, but his suppers of cold meat and salad were cheerful and pleasant; sometimes the cheerfulness (after a "wassail bowl") soared into noisy merriment. I remember one Christmas or New Year's evening, when we sat there till two or three o'clock in the morning, and when the jokes and stories and imitations so overcame me that I was nearly falling off my chair with laughter. This was mainly owing to the comic imitations of Coulson, who was usually so grave a man. Coulson knew everything. We used to refer to him as to an encyclopedia, so perpetually, indeed, that Hunt always spoke of him afterwards as "The Admirable Coulson." The *vis comica* left him for the most part in later life, when he became a distinguished lawyer.

Leigh Hunt was always in trouble about money; but he was seldom sad, and never sour. The prospect of poverty did not make much impression on him who never possessed wealth. Otherwise he would probably have pursued some regular laborious employment. He deceived himself, when he said that he could not understand accounts. He had a good logical head and great quickness, but he liked the tasks to which he devoted his life. He liked to display his worship for Spenser, to criticise poetry, and to write of May-day and of rural pleasures. I believe that he seldom if ever undertook a task to which he was originally disinclined. There is no doubt that some of his voluntaries became wearisome before completion, but the work was always commenced because it was attractive to him.

Hunt had a crotchet or theory about social intercourse (between the sexes), to which he never made any converts. He was at one time too frequently harping on this subject. This used to irritate Hazlitt, who said, "D—— him; it's always coming out like a rash. Why doesn't he write a book about it, and get rid of it." Hunt did not press these opinions upon any one to a pitch of offence. He himself led a very domestic and correct life. And I am bound to say that, during an intimacy of many (forty) years, I never heard him utter an oath, although they were then very common ; and I never heard from him an indelicate hint or allusion. Notwithstanding he indulged himself occasionally in pet words, some of which struck me as approaching almost to the vulgar. He was essentially a gentleman in conduct, in demeanor, in manner, in his consideration for others — indeed, in all things that constitute the material of a gentleman. He was very good tempered ; thoroughly easy tempered. He saw hosts of writers, of less ability than himself, outstripping him on the road to future success, yet I never heard from him a word that could be construed into jealousy or envy ; not even a murmur. This might have arisen partly from a want of susceptibility in his constitution ; not altogether from that stern power of self-conquest, which enables some men to subdue the rebellious instincts which give rise to envious passions.

Apart from this question, however, Leigh Hunt possessed a great fund of positive active kindness. He bestowed praise on the great and on the small with a liberal hand. He placed on record his liking for writers, who differed so materially from himself in merit, that the promulgation of this was likely to suggest a doubt as to the validity of his own pretensions. To persons whose ability was not yet admitted, or who had encountered enmity in letters, he was always generous, never taking the mean or ill-natured view, where the brighter might be adopted. Although he was a careful and just critic (never praising or blaming a book without reading it throughout), he always looked on the tender part of man's nature and on the pleasanter side of things.

He had no vanity, in the usually accepted meaning of the word. I mean, that he had not that exclusive vanity which rejects almost all things beyond self. He gave as well as received ; no one more willingly. He accepted praise less as a mark of respect from others, than as a delight of which all are entitled to partake, such as spring weather, the scent of flowers, or the flavor of wine. It is difficult to explain this ; it was like an absorbing property in the surface of the skin. Its possessor enjoys pleasure almost involuntarily, whilst another of colder or harder temperament is insensible to it. He had good, but not violent impulses. He was soon swayed, less by his convictions than by his affections. His mind had not much of the debating element in it. His smiles and tears were easy.

Yet Leigh Hunt was sometimes persistent in his opinions ; especially in reference to books and music which he loved. But his comparative estimates of authors were perhaps sometimes at

fault. He liked Milton more, and Spenser far
more, than Shakespeare. I never saw a volume
of that greatest of dramatists and poets in his
house; but the beloved Spenser was always there,
close at hand, for quotation or reference. I
suspect that his reading was not very extensive,
and that he therefore made up his mind upon too
confined a view. He became a critic and a pro-
nouncer of his own opinions too early. It is best
to begin life by becoming a disciple. Hunt was
never an under-graduate. He became a dispenser
of praise and blame too soon after his departure
from Christ's Hospital School.

He had not time to form and build up
opinions. They were in fact sometimes little
more than guesses, which had not been matured
into fixed ideas. It was too much the case
throughout his life. Hunt treated all people
fairly, yet seldom or never looked up to any one
with much respect; he treated all men as equals,
dissenting freely from their conclusions, however
laboriously formed, whenever they jarred with his
own thoughts. If I say his mind was feminine
rather than manly, I do not intend to speak
disrespectfully of his intellect, nor of the intellect
of women, which by nature is perhaps generally
equal to that of men.

Leigh Hunt had nothing of the dramatic faculty, and I do not consider that " The Legend of Florence " disproves this. But it does not stand in the foremost rank of his writings. He did not love the drama as he loved the " Faery Queen." Next to Spenser was his great and unfeigned love for music.

Of Keats I have little to record. I saw him only two or three times before his departure for Italy. I was introduced to him by Leigh Hunt, and found him very pleasant, and free from all affectation in manner and opinion. Indeed, it would be difficult to discover a man with a more bright and open countenance. He was always ready to hear and to reply; to discuss, to reason, to admit; and to join in serious talk or common gossip. It has been said that his poetry was affected and effeminate. I can only say that I never encountered a more manly and simple young man.

In person he was short, and had eyes large and wonderfully luminous, and a resolute bearing; not defiant, but well sustained. In common with thousands of others, I profess to be a great admirer of his poetry, which is charming and original; full of sentiment, full of beauty. Some persons prefer it to the verse of Shelley, which is

9*

less definite and picturesque, perhaps, but matchless in its resounding harmonies. As it is not necessary to enter into any invidious comparison between these two excellent poets, I content myself with testifying my great admiration for both.

Were it necessary, in this place, to characterize Keats as a writer, I should say that he was more intensely and exclusively poetical than any other. No one can read his poems (including Endymion and all others subsequently published) without feeling at once that he is communing with a great poet. There can be no mistake about his *quality*. It is above all doubt; and if, like Lucifer, he has not drawn after him a third part of the heavens, he has had a radiant train of followers, comprising (with the exception of the great name of Wordsworth) all who have since succeeded in distinguishing themselves in the same sphere of art.

WILLIAM GODWIN.

William Godwin, a small man, apparently of cold temperament, but abounding in literary energy, sprang to life after the blaze of the French Revolution. I feel some difficulty in offering an opinion about him. Mr. Thomas Campbell (the poet) had a cold, Scotch manner, but that was

merely the educated habit or manner of his country — cautious, canny. There was sap behind the
bark. If the oppression of the Poles or any other
flagrant enormity was brought before him, his
energy quickly flamed up. And he was also very
vivacious, not to say riotous, in his cups.

But Godwin was always the same ; very cold,
very selfish, very calculating. His philosophy,
such as it was, never generated pity or gratitude.
His sympathies and generosities and liberal qualities showed themselves only in print. His conduct towards Shelley was merely an endeavor to
extract from him as much money as was possible.
His conduct towards Mr. ——, whom I have heard
speak of it, in denying a pecuniary liability, because, as he said, " there was no witness to the
loan ; " his pedantic cavilling at his wife's unscien-
tific expression when dying, " Oh, Godwin, I am in
heaven ! " (expressive of her relief from extreme
pain), all indicate an unamiable character. I have
known several persons who were intimate with him,
none of whom ever pretended to endue him with a
single good quality. He was very pragmatic,
very sceptical of God and men and virtue. And
yet this man has in his study compiled fine rhetorical sentences, which strangers have been ready

to believe flowed warm from his heart. I have always thought him like one of those cold intellectual demons of whom we read in French and German stories, who come upon earth to do good to no one and harm to many.

THE " LONDON MAGAZINE."

I was invited to become a contributor to the "London Magazine" soon after its establishment in January, 1820. It was a work professing impartial and advocating liberal opinions. Mr. John Scott, former editor of the "Champion Newspaper," was the conductor; and Hazlitt, Mr. Cary, Charles Lamb, Allan Cunningham, and others formed the staff; and subsequently were added to it Mr. George Darley, Mr. John Hamilton Reynolds, Thomas Hood, T. de Quincey, Hartley Coleridge, and the too celebrated Thomas Griffiths Wainwright.

I have spoken already of Lamb and Hazlitt. Mr. John Scott had nothing about him which enables me to distinguish him much from other literary men. He was a shrewd and able writer, had great industry, and a considerable amount of critical taste; and was moreover a little irritable. He became involved, as is generally known, in a quarrel with Mr. Lockhart, which terminated to the dissatisfaction of both parties, and was followed by a duel with Mr. Lockhart's second, and the consequent death of Scott. In this latter affair, there is little doubt that Mr. Scott was the person entirely in fault. He was urged on by some busy friend, who would not permit him to be content with the result of the first quarrel. I have heard persons, who saw him in the interval, say that his uneasiness forced itself on every person's observation, when he referred to the first quarrel; and he was continually referring to it. Mr. Scott's contributions to the magazine consisted of elaborate articles on Mr. Wordsworth, Sir Walter Scott, Mr. Godwin, and other prominent authors of the day; and he also gave political articles to the work.

On Scott's death, the magazine remained without any ostensible editor, and passed from the proprietorship of Messrs. Baldwin, Cradock, and Joy (with whom it originated), into that of Messrs. Taylor and Hessey. Under these two firms it extended to ten volumes, and was of five years' duration. After that time, it was under the conduct of Mr. Henry Southern, and finally, I believe, went into other hands, and expired of inanition.

When Messrs. Taylor and Hessey assumed the management of the " London Magazine," they opened an office for the sale of it in Waterloo Place. Here most of the contributors met the proprietors once a month, at an excellent dinner given by the firm, and consulted and talked on literary matters, and enlarged their social sympathies. Here came Cunningham, and Lamb, and Reynolds, and Hood, and De Quincey, and others; once I think Hazlitt. Poor John Clare (the Northamptonshire peasant-poet) was there, full of wonder at London, which he had never seen before. Here came Lamb, always kind and genial, with author all cast off, and here also once came Mr. De Quincey, the famous opium-eater, by no means genial or unbending to the company around him. Lamb used, when he was able to do so, to sit by me; when he would say, " My boy, you will see me home to-night, I know."

Allan Cunningham, a stalwart man, very Scotch in aspect, was always ready to do a kind turn for any one. He was, in prose, a voluminous writer. His Scottish songs — some of which are excellent, and indeed not very unlike those of Burns — are by far his best gifts to the world. His other productions were not so good. He wrote long prose tales about Scottish life, which had not much interest for the English reader; and he took very extensive surveys of general literature and art. He did not fail in any of these subjects, for he took care to make himself sufficiently acquainted with his theme before he entered upon it. But his opinions appeared to be collected from others, rather than to have been formed by his own meditation. He was an excellent song-writer, and a kind and honorable man, and one could not help liking him better than authors of greater name and far greater pretensions.

The translator of Dante (the Rev. Henry Francis Cary) was the mildest and most amiable of men. The extreme gentleness of his face almost hurt its intelligence; yet he spoke well and with sufficient readiness on such subjects as he chose to discuss. He had a large acquaintance with Greek and Italian, French and English books. His ostensible means of living consisted of an office in the British Museum, where he was sub-librarian. His most important papers in the " London Maga-zine " were notices of the early French poets, with translations of passages in their works. These comprised verses from Clement Marot, Thie-baut, King of Navarre, Ronsard, Alain Chartier, and other well-known writers, of the twelfth, thirteenth, fourteenth, and fifteenth centuries. Mr. Cary was intimate chiefly with Charles Lamb (whom he sometimes entertained at dinner) and with George Darley, although he was kind and familiar with his other colleagues.

I am not competent to determine how far Mr. Cary's version of Dante affords an adequate view of the original Italian ; but I believe that the meaning of the " Divine Comedy " is on the whole ably and faithfully rendered ; as far, at least, as English blank verse can accurately represent Italian rhyme. Certainly Mr. Cary's lines are generally good (somewhat Miltonic, perhaps), and in some instances, as in the " Inferno," where the poem deals with Paolo and Francesca, and in other pathetic portions, the verse is graceful and touching. The task of embalming seven or eight hundred foreign names in tolerable English verse must have presented great difficulties. Mr. Cary was a scholar of much learning and vast industry, and was without an atom of pretension. One could not help being surprised into a little admiration, when we saw this accomplished man, who had traversed the ghostly mysteries of Dante, and who had made that high poet, together with Anacreon and (I think) Pindar, familiar to his countrymen, subside into the simple under-librarian of the British Museum; satisfied with the back instead of the soul of books. He exchanged frequent little courtesies with the workers on the " London Magazine " on equal terms, and was as unassuming as one of the humble neophytes of literature.

I need not descant on the works or character of Thomas Hood, whose life has been already written by his family, who loved him, and of course knew him well. He was an undoubted poet, and his merits are now universally acknowledged by those who are best acquainted with English verse. His first contribution to the " London Magazine " was in 1823, when he printed his poem of " Lycus the Centaur." His comic were more popular than his graver writings; but I myself prefer his serious verse, which alone calls out the greater qualities of a writer. Hood had a fine ear for metre, and exhibited . marvellous ingenuity in his rhymes. His labors consisted of writing verse, and his pastime in making puns and shooting sparrows. I have often wondered that he did not make this passerine sport the subject of an ode; for no one was more capable of jesting with his own peculiar-

ities than Thomas Hood. He married the sister of
John Hamilton Reynolds, a pleasant and very
lovable woman, who comforted and soothed him in
his last days, when they were clouding over. In
his fortunate time he possessed good spirits (at
least when he was in company), and these exhibited themselves in frequent puns and sly jokes. He
had a quiet face, the laughter lying hid behind its
gravity. Just before his death, when consumption
had mastered him, and the caprice of public favor
had much diminished his means of living, he bore
himself very independently.

Mr. John Hamilton Reynolds was lively, quick,
and witty. His contributions to the " London
Magazine " consisted chiefly of essays on character
and jocose articles. He also was the author of
some graceful poems, one of which extracted public commendation from Lord Byron. He was the
author of the " Garden of Florence," a poem
founded (like those of many other writers) upon
one of Boccaccio's stories. One of Mr. Reynolds'
smaller poems, which begins with a line like " Go
where the water glideth gently ever," often rises
up in my memory.

Mr. George Darley was a writer of considerable
power. He was — without possessing ill-nature —

of a sarcastic turn. Having an inveterate stam-
mer, he was thrown almost entirely out of society,
and this loneliness produced melancholy, and sometimes a little acerbity in his humor. He was once
tempted by this physical ailment to travel as far as
Edinburgh, to consult a professor of elocution who
professed to cure similar defects. The remedy,
which appeared to consist in causing his pupils or
patients to utter all their words in a sort of chant,
produced no permanently good effect. Darley was
well read in English literature; he wrote several
dramas; some (not very laudatory) criticisms;
and distinguished himself much by several educa-
tional books on mathematics. He was a member
of Trinity College, Dublin, where he became an
accomplished mathematician. He loved romance
and poetry most, however, and considered that he
stooped from his natural height when he quitted
the company of the beloved Muse to pay court to
Euclid.

I refrain from expatiating on Mr. Thomas de
Quincey. I did not like him, and I do not admire
those essays of his with which I am best acquainted.
He dined once at Taylor and Hessey's monthly
festivity, and I saw him once or twice elsewhere.
His paper entitled "Confessions of an Opium

Eater " is undoubtedly powerful writing; but his
" Reminiscences " and " Biographical Essays "
stand in a different predicament. These are in my
opinion often poor and without merit. I do not
know any instance in the writings of an author of
note comprehending so much pedantry, pretension
and impertinence. They are all divergence. Even
in the splenetic parts he cannot adhere to his subject; but must recede to some opinion of his own
which has no connection with the matter on hand,
or he refers to some classical or German author for
the sake of exhibiting his learning, or general
knowledge. His style therefore becomes wearisome, inconsequent, and parenthetical to an offen-
sive degree. He has written three essays on
Charles Lamb, two on Wordsworth, and he has
recorded his admiration of Coleridge in another.
In one of the papers on Lamb, after stating that
the " Essays of Elia " reflect the " stamp of the
writer's own character," he refers to other authors.
whose writings do and do not exhibit the same
quality. Amongst these is the well-known J. P.
Richter, in whom (he says) " the philosophy of
this interaction between the author as a human
agency and his theme as an intellectual re-agency
might best be studied." From him might be de-

rived many cases " illustrating boldly this absorption of the universal into the concrete." This is the way in which he perverts a simple idea.

The Biographical Essay on Charles Lamb is, however, remarkable principally for the author's sneers at and disparagement of Hazlitt. Mr. de Quincey and Hazlitt thought poorly of each other. Hazlitt pronounced verbally that the other would be good only " whilst the opium was trickling from his mouth," but he never published anything derogatory to the other's genius. De Quincey, on the other hand, seems to have forced opportunities for sneering at Hazlitt. For my own part, I think that the opinions of both were wrong ; Hazlitt in part, De Quincey altogether. It is not worth while entering into this quarrel ; but I observe that Mr. de Quincy denounces as defects in Hazlitt those qualities which he himself did not possess. If Hazlitt's sentences are occasionally too epigrammatic, his style had the great merit of directness and solidity. He never seems to have spun out his sentences from love of prolixity, nor to have foisted in his "little learning" upon all occasions, to fatigue and perplex his readers. Mr. de Quincey was certainly an able man ; and he was, I believe, liked and admired by those to whom he uncovered his more amiable qualities. But this exposition did not take place in London, where his attractions were not manifested. We had but a partial view of him.

There is in my opinion little of what is earnest in the works of Mr. de Quincey, except in his " Opium Eater." His three straggling essays on Charles Lamb, exceeding one hundred and eighty pages, contain scanty information about that charming writer. I do not think that he saw or knew much of Lamb. He says, " Not until 1823, did I know Charles Lamb thoroughly." Now, *I* knew Lamb in 1818, and was intimate with him and saw him continuously from that time through *all* the remainder of his life, until his death in 1834. Yet during the whole of that period I never saw Mr. de Quincey at Charles Lamb's house, and I never heard Lamb refer to him or mention his name upon any single occasion.

PART III.

——•——

UNPUBLISHED VERSES.

PART III.

UNPUBLISHED VERSES.

———◆———

Mr. Procter left among his papers a good many short pieces, which have not been printed in any edition of his poems. Of these, all but a few are given here, since it does not appear that they were withheld from the press for any reason but that some of them were personal; others mislaid, or forgotten, or written after the latest author's issue of the " English Songs."

————

Peace ! harm not thou the poet's fame,
Nor deem his life was lost in shame,
   Who, in our youth,
Fed us with music rare and wild,
Home thoughts and patriot love, and fill'd
   Our hearts with truth.

Better a thousand faults forgot,
Than wrong for once the poet's lot
   With hint or lie,
Who raised us from the trodden ground,
And gave us all the light he found
   In air or sky.

Better he rose on sightless wings,
To where the lost lark wildly sings,
   Hard by the sun,
Than drag him from his airy height.
What good, though thou couldst *quench* his
    light,
   Whose life is done?

Is it to show a child of Fame
Hath *something* of the common aim?
   Of hope? of fear?
Earth's human faults? its wild desires?
The ambition which the vulgar fires?
   Alas! all's clear.

Poor poets! There is little need
To prove ye are not free, indeed,
   From fault or stain!
Your weakness — still allied to worth —
Your halting rhymes (the critic's mirth!)
   Are all too plain.

A HAPPY GROUP.

I've traversed England : round and round
My long laborious course has bent :
From hurrying Dart to lazy Trent ;
Where'er the railway whistles sound ;
Where'er the electric words are sent.

Yet nowhere have I, wandering, known
A happier group than sits and sews,
From morning light to evening's close,
Within a smoke-beleaguered town,
Girt in by rivals, — haply foes.

No murmuring river meets the ear ;
No sward impearled by daisies springs ;
No rose-fed breezes whisper here ;
Yet wealth, beyond the wealth of kings,
Lies hid ; and here's a bird that sings

A sweet contented song, the while
The patient maidens sit and sew
In silence, or, 'midst whispers low,
They interchange a quiet smile,
As down the summer evenings flow.

Maid Marian weaves her threads of lace ;
Sibylla hangs with dreaming soul
O'er silken spray and eyelet hole ;
And Ruth, with blind but cheerful face,
Toils thro' the worsted like a mole.

Above, the ancient mother sits,
Rheumatic, yet preceptress still:
Tho' helpless all, she hath her will ;
Her humors, too, they flash by fits,
And sound in words that mean no ill.

A silver-clasped book the dame
Still reads ; the old large-lettered page
Is open, plain, and fit for age ;
From this she expoundeth praise and blame,
And future wonders doth presage.

Ah, patient poor, thrice-linked by love,
May heaven and beauteous earth entwine
Within your woof a golden line.
Be happy, as the skies above,
Where love is endless and divine.

MY GONDOLIER.

Gondolier, gondolier!
Sleepeth thy boat on the waters clear?
Ah, where is the false, false traitor flown,
Who vowed he would watch for the lady lone,
Till midnight dark, till dawn of day?
Ah, see! he cometh! Away, away!

Gondolier, gondolier!
Bear me over the waters clear,
And a lady's thanks and a purse of gold
Shall into thy palm be truly told,
As soon as on Padua's ground I stand,
Safe by my Knight of the Iron-hand!

Gondolier, gondolier!
Hast thou a child or a mother dear?
Hast thou a wife or a maiden true
Who watcheth thy boat o'er the waters blue?
Ah, think 'tis *she* whom thou now dost bear
To a firmer land and a freer air!

Gondolier, gondolier!
Bravely we fly o'er the waters clear!
Yet, open thy sail and woo the wind,
For we never should scorn a friend so kind.

On, on!   Who cometh from yon low land?
Ah, 'tis *he* — my Knight of the Iron-hand!

"MERRILY THE BROOK SINGETH."

Merrily the brook singeth
  As it roams along :
Overhead the lark trilleth
  Many a merry song ;
Round the mead the colt runneth
  In its frolic play ;
And the merry leaves are dancing
  In the sunny day.

  But, ah! the world is very wide,
  And hath both a dark and a sunny side ;
  And the light it gilds the palace tall,
  While the shadows hang on the cottage wall.

The wine upon the dean's table
  Sparkles like a star :
Where the city kings revel,
  Odors steam afar :
In his coach the peer rideth,
  Proud and free of care ;
And the jewelled dame reposeth
  In the perfumed air.

But, ah! the world is very wide,
And hath hovels for want, as homes for pride,
And the gaunt wolf hunger makes his den
Where man is starving amongst men.

Nobles, bishops, land-owners,
  Merchants (young and old),
There is something wrong, masters,
  In your piled gold :
There is something wrong, beadles,
  At the parish door :
God hath given earth, as heaven,
  Both to rich and poor.

  Ah! then, through all the world so wide,
  Let us share both the dark and the sunny
      side ;
  And right, the spirit, shall conquer wrong,
  And the story of life be a merry song.

FOR THE NIGHT REFUGE.

Hunger and cold! hunger and cold!
Look! Without pipes or trumps or drums,
But trampling down both the poor and the old,
The conqueror, terrible Winter, comes!

What had been even the Moscow fight,
What the Crimean deadly shore,
What Hohenlinden's guns by night,
Without the knife of the winter hoar?

Hunger and cold! hunger and cold!—
Give as the world has given to you!
Money and bread and words of gold!
Give!—if your heart be warm and true!

Look! here's a woman so thin and pale;
Give her a draught of the wine that's old.
Look! here's a man once young and hale,
Stumbling down to the churchyard mould.

Give! here's a mother, her breasts are dry,
Give! here's a ghastly child unfed,
Shelter and food as they pass you by;
Help! or their sleep is amongst the dead.

You, who give with a bosom warm,
And words all balm like the summer's breath,
May God shield *you* from the murdering storm,
And save you from want and a cruel death.

THE FIELD PREACHER.

They hunt me in alley and lane ; they have hunted
    me on to the moor.
I give them soft words in reply. I know what it
    is to endure.
I show them my Bible, and read, till they laugh at
    and stone me away.
It is night in the alleys and lanes ; but I know
    that there cometh the day.

I know what the good have endured : I know
    what a shepherd must bear,
Who tries to give help to his flock, and drive the
    foul mist from the air.
So here, on the moor, I will read the tale of the
    mercies of God :
I will try if the truth will arise, like a blossom that
    springs from the sod.

Christ's lesson (the one on the Mount) I will
    preach unto all that will hear.
What care if they stone me to death ? It is but to
    rest on a bier.
I abandon the trades of the world : I abandon the
    seeking of gold :
A light has come on me (in youth) : I will follow
    till life shall grow old,

10*   o

I will follow wherever it lead, to prison or pain
    tho' it be.
The fate that is written on high is the welcomest
    fortune to me.

THE BURIAL CLUB, 1839.

Soh ! — there's another gone,
    How purple he looks, — but wait !
We'll tumble him into his coffin ;
    And bury the body straight.

No one will see where the poison
    Has trickled and left its trace !
How curled up he is !   I wonder
    How the blue came into his face.

We'll find him a shroud for a shilling ;
    We'll cover the limbs up tight :
Who see him shall swear we are willing
    To do our duty to-night.

Dead !   That's a guinea for each :
    No need to spend aught on his meals ;
There's the little one — but she's a-dying ;
    And Connor, the boy, — but he steals.

I was once, I confess, chicken-hearted :
  His moans made me tremble and shrink :
But I thought of the club and the money,
  Grew bolder, and gave him the drink.

A SONG.

Take thou, where thou dost glide,
  This deep-dyed rose, O river !
And bear it to my bride
  And say " I love " for ever.

Take thou this lock of hair ;
  So may she love the giver,
Who loves and knows her fair
  Beyond the world, O river !

Where'er thy waters rove,
  Be thou my courier ever,
And murmur to my love,
  " I love " — no more, sweet river.

Now flow with speed, with mirth,
  And leave thy sweet song never :
Flow, flow, — like love on earth,
  Pure, bright, and swift, O river !

INSCRIPTION (FOR TWO SISTER TREES).

These trees now growing here, in freshest earth,
Memorials are of two small sisters' birth.
The slips from which they sprang and still spring
    free
Were cut in autumn from the self-same tree ;
And so each twain are sisters : we who now
Inscribe this tablet-stone have breathed a vow
That should our children die these trees shall fall.
Pray therefore from your hearts, sweet strangers
    all,
Pray gently, without end, that axe or knife
May never come, and cut the green twins' life,
But that, thro' all the seasons, sun and breeze
May nourish them by sure though slow degrees,
Till each (its century of summers past)
May sigh to drop its leaves and sleep at last.

IMPROBUS LABOR.

Labor ! labor, thro' the seasons,
    Every hour, every day !
Toil hath banish'd sports and pleasures,
    Healthy pastimes, far away.

Not a minute to trim my fancy!
   Scarce a minute to probe my mind!
And time runs, and I am sinking,
   Old, and weak, and deaf, and blind.

In the morn are dreams of labor;
   Labor still till set of sun;
Evening comes with scanty respite;
   Night — and not one good is won.
Formal phrases! — barren figures! —
   Sentence such as steam might turn!
What, from such laborious trifling,
   Can the human creature learn?

I remember — hopeful visions
   Since that time have fled away —
When wild autumn brought its leisure,
   And the sunshine summer day.
Now unseen the river wandereth,
   And the stars shine on their way;
Flowers may bloom; but I, poor laborer,
   With the worn-out year decay.

THE HEBREW PRIEST'S SONG.

I will raise my head from the dust;
   I will sing to the Lord a new song:
His words are as winds at night,
   His strength is beyond the strong.

Before the mountains arose,
  Before the stars of the sky
He was, and shall ever be;
  All else shall wither and die.

He gives us the breath of life
  And the cunning that need not stray;
He turns us from sloth and strife
  And pointeth the righteous way.

He is Lord of the hosts of heaven;
  He is Master of all below,
At His will the stars and the thunder speak,
  And the rose and the lily blow.

Beside Him His justice shines,
  And mercy and truth before;
By justice shall man be judged,
  By His truth and His worth shall soar.

Let us labor thro' day and night,
  Let us labor in sun and shade;
What is good in God the maker,
  Is good in the man He made.

THE GOLDEN FARMER.

Merrily laughs the farmer bold ;
   Many a wealthy hoard has he ;
Bottles of thirty summers old,
   Wine as rich as a wine may be :
And a buxom wife is upon his knee ;
   And low at his feet his children roll ;
Pain nor poverty, care nor fear,
   Trouble the Golden Farmer's soul.

Easily pleased, he smiles on all ;
   Friends he has over the county's bound ;
Scattered wherever you choose to call,
   Ready whenever the ale runs round ;
He moweth the grass, he tilleth the ground,
   Just in the old-fashioned farmer's way ;
And sleeps (what else can he do ? good man,)
   At the end of the long hard-toiling day.

He rideth a mare of the desert breed,
   Sinewy, strong, and as black as night ;
And some, who talk of her matchless speed,
   . Will swear she out-gallops the evening light ;
Now and then, when all goes right,
   The farmer he taketh the evening air,
Mounting his steed like a baron bold,
   And vanishing, faith, we scarce know where.

But envy, — what will it not do with man, —
    Some fellow, who hateth an honest fame,
Has tracked him again, and still again,
    And blackened the jovial farmer's name.
Once, when his neighbors met his eye,
    They laughed and put out the friendly hand ;
But now they mutter, and pass him by,
    And hint — what I never can understand.

I have drunk his ale, I have eaten his bread,
    I have laughed with him now for six long
        years,
And I know I shall love him, alive or dead,
    Whatever be other men's doubts or fears ;
Perhaps, — for he is not a Whig or a Tory,
    And therefore he has not a mighty friend, —
Some day, perhaps, they will trump up a story,
    And swear he has come to a shameful end.

      *   *   *   *   *

Alas! he is there — on the Bagshot moor ;
    An iron beneath his purple head ;
Under his foot no stirrup, nor floor
    To echo beneath his manly tread ;
His cheeks are pale, his jollity fled ;
    He is left alone with the scornful blast ;
Turning about in his creaking chains,
    A skeleton moral and text at last.

TO MY NIECE, MARIE DE VIRY.

Ma chère amie — these words are old,
Yet write them now in lines of gold,
And sing them too, in sounds more sweet
Than when June winds and roses meet,
For very dear is one to me,
Ma cherè amie — Ma chère Marie !

My friend has lived but two short years,
Has many smiles, has some few tears,
Tells fibs, too — with such pretty air,
You scarce would wish the truth were there;
Is passionate, wild, yet dear to me,
And thence I call her — chère amie !

Upon her heart, upon her head,
May genius, goodness, love be shed,
May joy with sweet content entwine,
May life like one short summer shine.
This is the wish I breathe for thee,
Ma chère amie — Ma chère Marie !

L'ONCLE.

TO EMILY DE VIRY.

You and yours, I know, will look
Sometimes in this little book,
Just because the book is mine,
And — for auld lang-syne.

So I send it, — with a whisper,
Bidding it take wing and flee, —
To you, and Albert, good and steady,
And — ma chère amie.

You will find in 't, now and then,
Verses fit for little men, '
And for little women too, —
Showing what they ought to do.
Not too much of this.   The rest
May be laid upon your breast,
As soft and doing little harm,
With — here and there, perhaps — a charm
For those friends of former times
Who still love me and my rhymes.

You have lost that eager gaze
Which you had in other days,
Yet your heart must be the same.
And I — alas, my little game
Is now played out and nothing won.
Altho' it is the set of sun,
And my hair is growing white
In the mournful evening light ;
And so — Good night !

THE RATIONALE OF LOVE.

Mother.

" Love not, my daughter of the golden hair !
Love not. In man dwells nought of true or fair,
To meet *thy* truth — to claim thy love or care."

Daughter.

" I love, O mother ! Like the morning sun,
Love thro' my pulsing veins doth shine and run.
I love, dear mother ! love — as thou hast done."

Mother.

" Stern, selfish, coarse, inconstant, nursed in strife,
Man strides a tyrant thro' the dream of life,
His friend a martyr, and his slave a wife."

Daughter.

" I love, O mother ! In the haunted air
I hear his voice, I see him brave and fair,
I hear, I see, I love him — everywhere."

MY BOOKS.

All round the room my silent servants wait, —
My friends in every season, bright and dim ;
Angels and seraphim
Come down and murmur to me, sweet and low,
And spirits of the skies all come and go
Early and late ;
From the old world's divine and distant date,
From the sublimer few,
Down to the poet who but yester-eve
Sang sweet and made us grieve,
All come, assembling here in order due.
And here I dwell with Poesy, my mate,
With Erato and all her vernal sighs,
Great Clio with her victories elate,
Or pale Urania's deep and starry eyes.
Oh friends, whom chance and change can never
          harm,
Whom Death the tyrant cannot doom to die,
Within whose folding soft eternal charm
I love to lie,
And meditate upon your verse that flows,
And fertilizes wheresoe'er it goes,
Whether   *   *   *   *

THE SONG OF ARIADNE.

Crown me with fire, O gods ! with rage —
  disdain —
With hate — with aught save love ; — for love
  must flee !
Teach me a curse to sear the false one's brain,
Who sought — won — wed, — and now — aban-
  dons me !

Now, whilst thy savage waves come howling
  home,
With prayers and spells I'll force thy help, O
  sea !
Mad music springs, they say, from out thy foam,
And, sometimes, charms (to death !) a wretch
  like me !

     Oh ! *why* will gentle thoughts arise
     To my heart and to my eyes ?
     Fill me with a woman's scorn !
     Let me not be *all* forlorn !

     I have loved ! how much — how well,
     There is one, alas ! might tell ;
     But he's with the summer flown,
     And hath left me — *all* alone !
         Alone ! to *die ;* alone !

TO THE PICTURE OF AN UNKNOWN PERSON.

COPIED FROM A PAINTING BY GIORGIONE.

O Queen! O Amazon! O lady-knight!
Or art thou some high-crowned cherub, — the
    proudest
Of all those starry ranks so fair and bright?
Where wast thou in the time of the angels' fight?
Was't not *thy* thunder-trumpet spoke the loudest
Of all that echoed on that dateless day?
When the red Moloch stained Heaven's azure way
With blood, and shook the everlasting air
With curses fiercer than the brave could bear?
Or wast thou pity-struck when he, the king,
Prince of the Morning (whose sweet smile could
    bring
Enchantment from her cave, and bend her still,
As the wind sways the cypress, to his will)
Was lightning-smitten, and had work to go
Through dusk and chaos to bewail his woe?
Oh! nameless — peerless — beautiful — what fame
Or nature (for thou hast some complete claim)
Hath chance assigned thee? Dost thou not reply?
Didst thou not utter once bright thoughts — and
    die?

Hast thou not faced the sun-light and sharp air,
And borne, as I have borne, joy and deep pain?
Or did'st thou plunge, like Day, from out the
　brain
Of the great painter who for once had gleams
Of Heaven, and, aiming to surpass his dreams,
Perished in madness and sublime despair?

VERSES IN MY OLD AGE.

Come, from the ends of the world,
　Winds of the air or sky,
Wherever the Thunder is hurled,
　Wherever the Lightnings fly!
Come with the bird on your bosom,
　(Linnet and lark that soars,)
Come with sweet Spring blossom,
　And the Sun from Southern shores.

I hate the snake Winter that creepeth,
　And poisons the buds of May,
I shout to the sun who sleepeth,
　And pray him awake to-day.
For the world is in want of his power,
　To vanquish the rebel storm,
All wait for his golden hour,
　Man, and beast, and worm.

Not only the seasons, failing,
　　Forsake their natural tone,
But Age droops onward, sailing,
　　And is lost in the seas unknown.
No wisdom redeemeth *his* sorrow,
　　For thought and strength are fled :
No hope enlightens to-morrow,
　　And the Past (so loved) is dead !
　　　　　　　　Dead ! — Dead !

EXHUMO.

Should you dream ever of the days departed, —
Of youth and morning, no more to return, —
Forget not me, so fond and passionate-hearted ;
　　　　Quiet at last reposing
　　　　Under the moss and fern.

There where the fretful lake in stormy weather
Comes circling round the reddening churchyard
　　pines
Rest, and call back the hours we lost together,
　　　　Talking of hope and soaring
　　　　Beyond poor earth's confines.

If, for those heavenly dreams too dimly sighted,
You became false, — why, 'tis a story old :

I, overcome by pain, and unrequited,
  Faded at last, and slumber
  Under the autumn mould.

Farewell, farewell !   No longer plighted lovers
Doomed for a day to sigh for sweet return :
One lives, indeed ; one heart the green earth
 covers, —
  Quiet at last, reposing
  Under the moss and fern.

11   P

PART IV.

———◆———

LETTERS FROM LITERARY FRIENDS.

PART IV.

LETTERS FROM LITERARY FRIENDS.

————•————

From LORD BYRON.

Pisa, 1822.

YOUR friend Captain Medwin is at this moment with me. . . . The story in " Blackwood " (which I have only just heard) is utterly false. I have had no geese (not even one on Michaelmas Day), and I should neither be such a fool nor buffoon as to baptize them if I had. I always thought highly of the dramatic specimens, and look upon " Mirandola " as a work of very great promise and deserved success. It is strange that Mr. Murray has not thought it worth his while to mention (that is, if you know him), that I expressly wrote to him my regret that I had not been aware of " Mirandola " at the date of the preface to " The Doge," etc. The latter work was sent to England in the summer of 1820, and " Mirandola " not announced till the winter following.   The first time I saw it mentioned was in a newspaper, many months after my own MS. had been sent to Albemarle Street. I never received the copy from the author, but a single copy sent from the bookseller as his own. Had I been aware of your tragedy (although it is a matter of not the least consequence to you), I should certainly *not* have omitted to insert your name with those of the other writers who still do honor to the drama.

My own notions on the subject of the English drama altogether are so very different from the popular ideas of the day, that we differ essentially (as indeed I do from our whole English literati) upon that topic ; but I do not contend that I am in the right.   I merely say that such is my opinion — and as it is a solitary one, it can do no great harm.

But this does not prevent me from doing justice to the *power* of those who adopt a different system.

I wish you every success, both on and off the stage, and am very truly your old schoolfellow and well wisher.

Yours, etc.,

BYRON.

P. S. I should feel it as a compliment if I could

have a copy of your new volume — sent by the post; it will reach me more quickly, and you need not have any remorse about the postage, as I am in the habit of having books so sent.

I, too, have been writing on the *Deluge;* but it is on *Noah!* I wonder if our thoughts *hit:* most probably.

From LORD BYRON.

Genoa, March 5th, 1823.

MY DEAR BARRY, — I have just got your poem and letter, of which more anon. You must blame the post and not *me*, for I wrote and sent to the address indicated a very long answer to your letter of a year ago — true, upon my honor! so much so, that I rather wondered at having heard no further from you; not that it required notice in itself — but merely as the link of as much correspondence as you chose to tie to it. Why don't you try the drama again? there is your *forte*, and you should set to work seriously; you will have the field to yourself, and are fully able to keep it.

As for myself — neither my way of thinking on the subject as an art — nor probably my powers — are at all adapted for the English drama — nor

did I ever think that they were. With regard to
" Don Juan," there are nine cantos, seven of which
are in England. The reason of the delay is a quarrel with Murray (on Hunt's account originally)
and a demur with the *trade* in general — excited
by the Arimaspian of Albemarle Street. The said
John M., Esq., who is powerful in his way and
in his wrath, has done and will do all that he can
to perplex or impede. As to what D. J. may do
in England — you will see. If you had had the
experience which I have had of the *grande monde*
in that and other countries, you would be aware
that there is no society so intrinsically (though
hypocritically) *intrigante* and profligate as English
high life.

I speak what I do know — from what I have
seen and *felt personally* in my youth — from what
I have undergone and been made to undergo —
and from what I know of the whole scene in general, by my own experience, and that of others ;
and my acquaintance was somewhat extensive. I
speak of seven years ago and more ; it may be
bettered now.

In no other country would the Queen's and
similiar trials have been *publicly* tolerated a moment.

They mistake the object of "Don Juan," which is nothing but a satire on affectations of all kinds, mixed with some relief of serious feeling and description. At least this is the object, and it will not be easy to bully me from "the farce of my humor."

I have prosed thus far in answer to your inquiry. "Patience and shuffle the cards." L—— H——, who is resident in this district, has carried off your "Flood" (by the way, we had one of our own this winter, which carried away bridges, cattle, and Christians) before I had time to read it. What little I gleaned I liked extremely. Moore has allowed the priests to menace his angels into Mahometans — a concession which I suspect will not stand him in stead. They will merely boast that they have threatened him out of his propriety. As to "The Liberal," I do not know how it is going on ; but all my friends of all parties have made a portentous outcry against the whole publication, and so continue, which is a great encouragement. However, my conscience acquits me of the motives attributed to me by the serviles of Government. What *I* have done to displease my aristocratic connections I can quite understand — in this matter ; but what the two

11*

H——'s are guilty of to sanction their invectives
is not quite so clear.

We have only seen the first number hitherto.

I hope that you are better. I am far from
well myself; but I won't make this a medical
epistle.

Write — when disposed — and tell of your
doings and intentions.

Am yours very truly,

N. B.

From Mr. Rogers.

Oct. 12*th*, 1824.

My dear Sir, — I congratulate you from my
heart; you have done what every wise and good
man must wish to do, or regret that he had not
done. That you may live long and happy, and
bequeath your name and your fame to your
children's children, is my sincere and earnest
prayer.

Ever yours most truly,

Saml. Rogers.

When I return to town, which will be very
soon, I shall not fail to remind you of your
promise.

From the REV. W. L. BOWLES.

March 28*th*, 1824.

DEAR SIR, — Mr. Grimani brought me your letter yesterday. I should have been most happy to have taken him to Bowood, but the whole family is in town, and all the pictures in canvas coverings, till Lord Lansdowne's return. I would have given your friend an introduction to Lord Suffolk, but he had already seen him and his fine collection. He has also a letter for Mr. Methuen of Corsham and Sir Richard Hoare, otherwise I would have taken care he should have every facility of giving an account of their collections. I have given him a note to Mr. Wiltshire, near Bath, ' who has the finest Gainsboroughs in England. There is no other gentleman in this neighborhood who has any pictures worth seeing.

As to the subject between me and Campbell, be assured, dear sir, there is " no intermediate ground." If my propositions *are* true, they are true in all their relations; and I am certain that the more they are examined fairly, and in the spirit of ingenuous and *liberal* discussion, the more they will be found as immutable as nature and as firm as truth.

The argument, divested of misrepresentations and verbal cavils, lies in a nutshell.

1st. Nature and *passions* furnish the grandest *materials*, the noblest subjects for poetry — ergo,

2nd. He is the *greatest poet* who has used these materials most successfully; in other words, he who has *treated the greatest subjects in the best and greatest manner is the greatest poet* — ergo,

Homer, Milton, Shakespeare, Sophocles, etc., are the greatest. Not Pope or any poet who has chiefly treated subjects less intrinsically sublime, or less adapted to the highest order of the poetical art.

Can you find a *flaw* in these obvious principles? Can you find any intermediate ground? From these points, or *axioms*, I have never wavered. To attack them, you must alter them in some way or other, as Campbell and Byron have done; but Byron has been beat back in every point, and he knows it, and is too high-minded not to admit it. Campbell had not considered the subject, for he surely could not suppose that any one but a goose would confine his ideas of poetry to descriptions of outward *nature*. But all art is nature when it is connected with moral associations, as the *Ruins of Athens*, or when it is rendered more poetical by *picturesque* adjuncts from nature, as a sailing ship. (*This* Campbell did not perceive.) Or when the poet, contemplating a specific work of art, leaves the marble or canvas and goes himself directly to the statuary, first great archetype, as you have done finely when you say of Theseus:

" And struck him — into marble ! "

Nature, as Pope himself says, is the end, the source, and *test* in these and all instances. I hope you will call at Hurst and Robinson's, who will give you my " Novissima " poetical criticism, in which I have put together the whole controversy. I am particularly anxious you should read the preface, and the summing up at the end, where I have even condescended to cope with an unprincipled perverter and despicable verbal quibbler. At all events, I am sure of meeting gentlemanly conduct and gentlemanly language from yourself.

Believe me very sincerely,

W. BOWLES.

To B. W. PROCTER,
10, *Francis Street, Gower Street.*

With respect to faculties of a poet, if it be said

" nature may furnish the noblest materials for poetry, but it requires the greatest genius to make use of them," this would be to say nothing to my question ; the poet's powers are all along presupposed. I have particularly guarded against this point. Homer, Shakespeare and Milton have made the finest use of these nobler materials. They therefore stand the first of their order. But answer this question yourself: — Would these very poets with the same faculties have stood as high and on a basis as *eternal* as that on which they now stand, if instead of tragedies and epic poems, they had written *moral* poems and satires ? Examine their works and see in which they shine most ? art or nature, local manners or eternal passions ? The question answers itself. I would rest the truth of my general *principles* on this *alone*.

From Sir Thomas Lawrence.

Russell Square, October 18*th*, 1824.

My dear Sir, — Allow me to offer you my sincere congratulations on your marriage, and to thank you for a flattering proof of your regard, in your sending me that customary present, which is usually claimed by long intimacy or near connection. Permit a very true esteem and admiration to take their place, as I have as full right to it as the oldest of your friends. I hope it will not be long after your return that you introduce me to a lady whose pleasing form and elegant manners I have before admired, and the known worth of whose family would dignify even higher claims than those it has so happily rewarded. I beg you to present my respects to Mrs. Procter, and have the pleasure to remain,

My dear Sir,

Most faithfully yours,

THOS. LAWRENCE.

From MR. JEFFREY.

Edinburgh, 4th January, 1824.

MY DEAR SIR, — I hope you have not entirely forgotten your *poetical article*. I am obliged feelingly to remember it, by the recurrence of my quarter day, and the usual *deficit* of supplies from my perfidious auxiliars. I am rather more than usually annoyed this time, however, because I find that I shall be obliged to run up to town at the early meeting of Parliament, on certain weighty official cases, and must, if possible, get my new

number of the "Review" afloat — or, at least,
fairly on the stocks, before I move. Do think of
me, therefore, and pray let me have comfortable
tidings as soon as possible.

I have only time to-day for this momentary
flash, though I should like extremely to have a
little quiet chat with you. We are all quite well,
and, for prose people, tolerably happy.

Mrs. J—— and I talk of you very often, and
wonder very innocently whether you really intend ever to come and take us in these inclement
regions.

My little girl reads your books, and says that
some of them are very pretty, though not to be
compared to Miss Edgeworth's "Simple Susan,"
and some other favorite legends. By-and-by she
will know better. God bless you. Remember me
sometimes at your leisure, and rely always on our
kindest remembrance.

Very affectionately yours,

F. JEFFREY.

I *must* have your paper, if for next number,
before the end of this month; and the sooner the
better.

I had just written this when I got your note;

and shall be most happy to see you as soon as you can come.

From MR. JEFFREY.

MY DEAR SIR, — As we set out for Scotland early to-morrow morning, I think it very uncertain whether I shall have the good luck to see you before I go; and therefore take this way of reminding you of the reliance I have on your helping me with a poetical article for the next number of the " Review," which I must bring out in the course of October, and for which my long absence has left me villanously unprovided. I know your kindness will induce you to make all the exertion you conveniently can to relieve me in this emergency, and shall only add that the sooner I can receive your contribution, it will be the more acceptable.

We have made a long and active tour, and seen a great deal which we shall long remember. It will be a singular delight to me to talk it all over to you some quiet autumn day at Edinburgh. Must it be next year and not this? If you are half as active as I am you will say — *this*.

We have all come back, in perfect health, very glad to be at home again, and thinking, at least, as

kindly as ever of our old friends. I reckon you
among the number, by a safe anticipation. God
bless you. I am in a bustle this morning, and
cannot indulge in any chat.

Very faithfully yours,

F. JEFFREY.

From MR. JEFFREY.

Craigcrook, 19th October, 1824.

MY DEAR SIR, — I am very sensible of your
kindness in giving me so early an opportunity of
congratulating you ; and very sorry that in consequence of my absence in the north I have not,
till now, been able to avail myself of it.

I do wish you joy, however, with all my heart;
and I feel assured that you will be a very happy
man. We shall hear no more, I take it, of your
nerves and your regimen, your weak spirits, or
your weak stomach.

I am half afraid that, seeing the numerous
things you will now bid adieu to, poetry may be
included; but I hope not.

I do not fear that you will bid adieu to your
friends — even the distant ones ; but I trust that,
to avoid hazards, you will bring Mrs. Procter
down here next summer, when Mrs. J—— and I

will be most happy to receive her, and make you, at last, a little acquainted with Scotland.

I am delighted to hear that your paper on poetry is in such forwardness, and hope you will be able to let me have it for the number which I must send forth in about a month after this time. I neither forgot nor despaired of you; but I do hate to dun benefactors, or use the language of an editor to those to whose kindness I am indebted.

Not hearing how you were employed, I did sometimes think you lazy, and sometimes feared you were ill; but the step you have just taken explains and makes amends for everything.

We have had a rambling summer, though scarcely at all out of Scotland. We were, lately, a fortnight at Loch Lomond, and were glad to find that our own hills and lakes were not at all injured by recollections of Switzerland.

It is not improbable that I may be in town in the spring; but I expect to hear often from you before that time.

Believe me always,

Very affectionately yours,

F. JEFFREY.

I am very much gratified by your project of a

paper on the " Drawings of Old Masters," but it is very true that I am anxious to have the other out of your hands — before they are turned to such ticklish matters.

From MR. JEFFREY.

Edinburgh, 12th May, 1826.

MY DEAR SIR, — I have lost sight of you for a long time, and I am afraid very much by my own fault; but I am a sadly irregular, forgetful person, and you must forgive me, for I never forget you, or cease to think kindly of you. But I have no leisure, and when I want to write to you I cannot find your address, or I am hurried away to a trial or a consultation, or obliged to scramble up a review, or tempted to write till it is too late. Then, my little girl has had the measles, and the bankruptcy of our publishers has plagued me in many ways; and Mrs. J.'s brother has been dying, and my own nerves have been shaken, and altogether I have had many apologies. But now, will you send me an article for my next number; that is to say, before the middle of June. You know you promised me half a dozen, half a year ago; and one of them is half written, and you cannot do better in short than finish it off now and despatch it to me by the mail. Then secondly, will you come and see me this summer? — I mean with Mrs. Procter, and stay a good while — and I will go with you, if I possibly can, to the Highlands, and at all events we will sit up late at Craigcrook and talk of poetry and virtue, and make ourselves happy in spite of fate and fortune. Now, these are my proposals for you, and I have no time to-day to say more, for it is the first day of our term, and I have fifty things to attend to which have been almost as long forgotten as my duty to you; and I only write now because in rummaging for something else I have fallen upon an old letter of yours with your address. Perhaps an old one too is it; and after reading I couldn't rest till I had tried to make my peace with you and to bring you back to a sense of your duties.

And so God bless you. . . . But still I want a lift from you.

Very affectionately yours,
F. JEFFREY.

Can you tell me anything of our ancient ally, Hazlitt?

From BEDDOES.

Bristol, March 3rd, 1824.

DEAR PROCTER, — I have just been reading your epistle to our Ajax Flagellifer, the bloody John Lacy : * on one point, where he is most vulnerable, you have omitted to place your sting. I mean his palpable ignorance of the Elizabethans and many other dramatic writers of this and preceding times, with whom he ought to have formed at least a nodding acquaintance before he offered himself as physician to Melpomene.

About Shakespeare you don't say enough. He was an incarnation of nature ; and you might just as well attempt to remodel the seasons, and the laws of life and death, as to alter " one jot or tittle " of his eternal thoughts. " A star " you call him. If he was a star, all the other stage scribblers can hardly be considered a constellation of brass buttons.

I say he was an universe, and all material existence with its excellences and defects was reflected in shadowy thought upon the crystal waters of his imagination, ever glorified as they

* George Darley, in the " London Magazine."

were by the sleepless sun of his golden intellect. And this imaginary universe had its seasons and changes, its harmonies and its discords, as well as the dirty reality. On the snow-maned necks of its winter hurricanes rode madness, despair, and "empty death, with the winds whistling through the white grating of his sides;" its summer of poetry glistening through the drops of pity; and its solemn and melancholy autumn breathing deep melody among the "sere and yellow leaves" of thunder-stricken life, etc., etc. (See Charles Phillips's speeches and X. Y. Z. for the completing furbelow of this paragraph.)

By the third scene of the fourth act of "Macbeth," I conclude that you mean the dialogue between Malcolm and Macduff, which is only part of the scene; for the latter part, from the entrance of Rosse, is of course necessary to create an interest in the destined avenger of Duncan, as well as to set the last edge to our hatred of the usurper. The Doctor's speech is merely a compliment to the "right divine" of people in turreted night-caps to cure sores a little more expeditiously than Dr. Solomons, and is, too, a little bit of smooth chat, to show by Macduff's manner that he has not yet heard of his wife's murder.

I hope Guzman has grown since I saw him, and has improved in voice. I shall be in London in about a week, and hope to find you in your Franciscan eyrie, singing among the red-brick boughs, and laying tragedy-eggs for Covent Garden Market.

So you " think this last author will do something extraordinary ; " so do I too. I should not at all wonder if he was to be plucked after his degree ; which would be quite delightful and new.

When does Fitzgerald publish his tragedy ?

This March wind has blown all my sense away, and so farewell.

Ever yours,

T. L. BEDDOES.

From FREILIGRATH.

10, Moorgate Street, Thursday.

MY DEAR SIR, — I am much obliged to you for the kind communication of Mr. Milnes' noble and splendid poem. It was still unknown to me ; and the pleasure to receive it written by your hand was, of course, an augmented one. If I shall ever translate it into German, I do not know as yet. The fact is, that (now a year ago) I made myself a poem describing the *outward* struggles of genius, with the same sympathy and, strange to say, in the same metre in which Mr. Milnes' glorious verses present such a striking picture of the inward sufferings of an elevated mind. Perhaps you have seen my poem in Mrs. Howitt's beautiful translation (towards the end of her new volume, and before, in the " People's Journal" and the " Athenæum ") ; and if so, you will only think it wise in me not to challenge my countrymen's criticism by giving them a translation of English verses, treating a similar subject in a way so very superior to my own feeble attempt. At all events, it has made me happy to coincide with Mr. Milnes in this manner, and I love and revere him the more for it. I must apologize for not having written to you sooner. To excuse oneself with want of time sounds so very stale, and yet I am but too much entitled to this most trivial of all excuses. With kindest regards to you and yours from Mrs. Freiligrath and myself,

I remain, dear Sir,

Yours very truly,

F. FREILIGRATH.

12

From BEDDOES.

October 9th, 1826.

MY DEAR PROCTER, — This Göttingen life is little productive of epistolary materials or of any adventure interesting beyond the town walls; and I have not been six miles from the circuit of these during the last year. However, I meditate and must perform a pilgrimage to Dresden, for the sake of its pictures, and then I hope to pick out a few plums to communicate to you. These matters, I take it for granted, retain their interest for you, because I have a lingering attachment to them, and in sincerity I acknowledge that you possess a truer and more steady feeling for the beautiful in imagination ; and the law-studies will probably only compress and concentrate it. You will give me leave to believe that you will not and cannot entirely abandon the studies and labors which have many years pretty exclusively possessed you, and by which you have obtained a distinguished reputation ; and if you do not, I shall take it. Me you safely regard as one banished from a service to which he was not adapted, but who has still a lingering affection for the land of dreams ; as yet, at least, not far enough in the journey of science to have lost sight of the old two-topped hill. I wish, indeed, that the times were more favorable to the cultivators of dramatic literature, which from a thousand causes appears to be more and more degraded from its original dignity and value among the fine arts. And yet I believe that the destined man would break through all difficulties and re-establish what ought to be the most distinguished department of our poetic literature; but perhaps enough has already been done, and we ought to be content with what times past have laid up for us. If literature has fallen into bad hands in England, it is little worse off than in Germany, for living and active are few writers above a secondary rank, and they almost unknown beyond the shadow of the double-eagle's wings.

Jean Paul is lately dead, and a new edition of his voluminous writings is proceeding from the press.

I have read little of his, and that little has pleased me less. In his happier moods he resembles Elia, but in general he is little better than a pedantical punster.

Tieck has made a good little story by threading together the few facts we have of Marlowe's life, and an English translation is advertised by a Leipzig bookseller, probably by himself. When it appears I shall send it to you by the first opportunity, without waiting for your order.

A quantity of our modern indifferent fellows have been cheaply reprinted by different speculating booksellers. It is a pity they have no good selector, who could spare them the pains of recondemning paper and print to the re-awaking of such trash. It would be as reasonable of dyers to reprint the London waistcoats and breeches of 1810 or '16; for a pattern and a poem of this sort are equally long-lived, and deserve to be so.

In the neighborhood is a little lake, See-Burger-See. We went there botanizing a few weeks ago, and were entertained by our boatman with a genuine legend. A castle had formerly stood on the edge of the water, and the ruins of it still exist on the rocks and under the waves. It was formerly inhabited by a knight who had a confidential cock and a prying servant. Once a month the master, to keep his ears awake to the language of his crowing oracle, partook of a mysterious dish; and it was decreed that whenever a second pair of ears were able to receive and comprehend Chanticleer's conversation, the castle should fall. At last, then, the servant removed the cover of the monthly viand and found a snake under it: he tasted some of this broiled worm of the tree of knowledge, and was from that day forth an eavesdropper of the confidential twitters in sparrows' nests and hencoops. The prophetic cock soon began to use fowl language, and proclaim the approaching downfall of the towers of ——burg. The servant who had translated colloquies between fly and fly, bee and flower, did not fail to comprehend the warning; rushed to his master, who was already on his horse and riding out of the castle gate: the walls tumbled, the towers bowed, the groom rushed after his master and seized the horse's tail; the knight plunged his spurs into the sides of his steed, leapt to land, and left his treacherous servant among the waves and ruins.

Here are also the Gleichen, two castles belonging to the family of Ernst von Gleichen, famous for having two wives: W. Scott has told the story somewhere. A grave is shown at Erfurt as containing the relics of the three, and at one of his castles a large bed; but it appears that this three-headed matrimony is fictitious and altogether unsupported by historical documents. These castles overlook a prettyish valley, which was a favorite haunt of poor Bürger the ballad-writer. He was a private teacher in Göttingen, and probably starved or at all events hastened through the gates of death by poverty and care. Schiller was supposed to be envious of him, and did him a good deal of mischief by ill-natured criticism; but Bürger had more notion of the right translunary thing than his reviewer. About Weber? What grief at the death? His fellow countrymen and fellow fiddlers were well-pleased with his burial or intended burial honors.

I wish you joy of Sir R. G——'s being out of the way; you may sit upon a woolsack yet. Was it to fill your sheet that you sent a good deal of advice or remonstrance in your last to me? Perhaps you forget it. I only mention it to observe that it is a little singular that a dramatic writer, a person who has observed and knows something of human character, should take the trouble to attempt corrections of the incorrigible, and pour so much oil upon a fire by way of extinguishing it. Allow me to say that you are mistaken if you think I wilfully affect any humor; even that of affecting nothing. I always make a point of agreeing with everything that a fool pleases to assert in conversation, and only combat assertions or opinions of a person for whom I have respect. *Verbum sap.* You people in England have a pretty false notion of the German character, and flatter yourselves with your peculiar and invincible insular self-complacency that you know all about it: for national vanity I believe after all you are unequalled. The Frenchman rests his boast on the military glories of *la grande nation;* the German smokes a contemptuous pipe over the philosophical works of his neighbors; but the Englishman will monopolize all honorable feeling, all gentle breeding, all domestic virtue, and indeed has ever been the best puritan. Is the revolution in the " Quarterly " true? The last number we had here did smack somewhat of " Blackwood." Present my best compliments to Mrs. Procter, and don't let your answer be as dull as this.

Yours,

T. L. BEDDOES.

Recollect I write from Göttingen.

" Death's Jest Book " is finished in the rough, and I will endeavor to write it out and send it to you before Easter: at all events I think parts of it will somewhat amuse you: ὁι πολλοὶ will find it quite indigestible. W. A. Schlegel is professor at Bonn, a ten years old Prussian university on the

Rhine. His brother Friedrich is in Austria, and writes puffs for the Holy Alliance. No Austrian is allowed to study here — Göttingen is so famous for liberality.

I intend to study Arabic and Anglo-Saxon soon.

I have just bought three salamanders. They are pretty, fat, yellow and black reptiles, that live here in the ruins of an old castle in the neighborhood; on the Hartz I hear they are larger. It is not a bad retributory metempsychosis for the soul of a bullying knight.

From BEDDOES.

19th April, 1829.

MY DEAR PROCTER, — Accept my thanks for the patience and attention with which you have read my MS., and for the manner in which you have spoken of it. I fear that if you had expressed your disapprobation of some of it still more strongly, I should have been obliged to confess that you were right. If you, as I have cause to apprehend, are not too well engaged in other and more substantial pursuits, you would oblige me still more by specifying the scenes and larger passages which should be erased (that is to say, if

I am to let any considerable part remain as it is, for perhaps it might take less time to enumerate such bits as might be retained). For of the three classes of defects which you mention — obscurity, conceits, and mysticism, — I am afraid I am blind to the first and last, as I may be supposed to have associated a certain train of ideas to a certain mode of expressing them, and my four German years may have a little impaired my English style; and to the second I am, alas! a little partial, for Cowley was the first poetical writer whom I learned to understand. I will, then, do my best for the Play this summer; in the autumn I return to London, and then we will see what can be done. I confess to being idle and careless enough in these matters, for one reason, because I often very shrewdly suspect that I have no real poetical call.

I would write more songs if I could, but I can't manage rhyme well or easily. I very seldom get a glimpse of the right sort of idea in the right light for a song; and eleven out of the dozen are always good for nothing. If I could rhyme well and order complicated verse harmoniously, I would try odes; but it's too difficult.

Am I right in supposing that you would denounce and order to be rewritten all the prose scenes and passages? — almost all the first and second, great part of the third act. Much of the two principal scenes of the fourth and the fifth to be strengthened, and its opportunities better worked on.

But you see this is no trifle, though I believe it ought to be done. Can you tell me whether Vondel's "Lucifer" has been translated? It is a tragedy somewhat in the form of "Seneca." J. von Vondel was born at Cologne, 1587 (according to van Rampen), and "Lucifer" published in 1654.

Milton, born in 1608, published "Paradise Lost" 1667.

It is to me very unlikely that Milton should have been acquainted with the Dutch language, for Latin was the learned language in Holland long after this period, and M—— was Cromwell's Latin secretary; therefore, if he had any business with the Dutch, he would not have transacted it unnecessarily in their language, and I do not recollect that he visited Holland in his travels; if he had, he would hardly have gone further than learned Leyden. Both on this account and because I am rather partial to Holland and the Dutch (for their doings against Spain, their toleration, their (old) liberty of the press, and their literature wonderfully rich for so small a people), I was very much pleased and struck on finding two lines in Vondel's " Lucifer," which I translate literally :

" And rather the first prince at an inferior court,
Than in the blessed light the second or still less."

"LUCIFER." Act II.

Does it not seem as if at certain periods of the world some secret influence in nature was acting universally on the spirit of mankind, and predisposing it to the culture of certain sciences or arts, and leading it to the discovery even of certain special ideas and facts in these ? I do not know whether the authors of philosophies of history have as yet made this observation, but it is sufficiently obvious, and might be supported by numerous instances. So in our times Scheele and Priestley ; the former in Sweden a few weeks later than P—— discovered oxygen gas. A little time before we have half-a-dozen candidates for the title of appliers of the power of steam in mechanics, etc. Middleton's " Witch " and " Macbeth " present in the lyrical parts so close a similarity, that one can hardly doubt of the existence here of imitation on one side. I cannot but think that M—— was the plagiarist, and that some error

must have occurred with regard to the dates of the
two pieces.　The King of Bavaria has commenced
poet, and a very sorry one he appears to be from
the newspaper extracts.　Kings as well as cobblers
should keep to their craft — and Louis is a very
reputable king ; but still every inch a king, as you
may see from his having made Thorwaldsen a
Knight of the Bavarian Crown!

That you may see that I am not the only careless dramatist going, I quote you three lines from
Oehlenschläger's new play, the "Norseman in
Constantinople."　"Ha!" his great, strapping,
tragic hero says in rage and despair :

> " Ha! knew the porkers what the old boar suffers,
>   They would raise up a dismal grunt and straight
>   Free him from torture."

This is as literally translated as possible ; and do
not disbelieve me if it should not happen to be in
the German translation, which, of course, is more
likely to be in London than the Danish original.
I have it from the latter ; probably it is not in the
German, which I have not seen.　Moreover,
Oehlenschläger is one of the very first of con-
tinental dramatists, perhaps the first, far above
Müllner, Grillparzer, Raupach, Immermann, etc.

I will sacrifice my raven to you; but my crocky is really very dear to me; and so, I dare say, was Oehlenschläger's pig-sty metaphor to him.

Yours ever,

T. L. BEDDOES.

From BEDDOES.

Milan, June 8th.

DEAR PROCTER, — If I do not dream, this is the city of Sforza, and to-day I have seen a picture of his wife by Leonardo da Vinci. Paris, Lyons, Turin and Novara, and beautiful Chambéry in its bed of vines, they have passed before me like the Drury Lane Diorama, and I almost doubt whether I have been sitting in the second tier or on the top of the diligence. Paris is far preferable to London as a place of amusement, and the manner of the lower orders is strikingly superior to that of their island equals. I saw the opera; the ballet much better than ours, but the music was French: the house is not nearly so commodious or elegant as Drury Lane, and the painting and mechanism of their scenery is not so dexterous and brilliant. The Teatro della Scala in this city I have not yet

seen ; it is considered only inferior to the San
Carlo at Naples. Savoy, from the French frontier
to Chambéry, is the most beautiful country I have
yet seen ; nothing between the Alps and Milan is
equally rich, varied, and delightful. Towards the
Alps the vines grow thinner, and give place at first
to corn, then to ragged herbage, and finally mother
earth hides her head under a coverlid of snow ;
and with their country and climate change the
inhabitants. You have the goitred and the crétins
instead of the Savoyard of gentle manners and
frank countenance. On the frontiers of fertile
Italy they brought us a salad of dandelions at
dinner.

June 9th. — Since I began this letter I have
been to the top of the cathedral, and in the pit of
the Teatro della Scala. The former is the finest
church externally which I have seen ; but the
interior of Westminster's old Abbey is triumphant
over the marble simplicity of the Milanese's
concave. The roof is finished with pinnacles and
battlements of white marble of a workmanship as
exquisite as if it were in ivory. From the summit,
all the rich country from Alp to Apennine, river
and hill and wood, the cool lakes and the vine-
yards of an ardent green, lay themselves at

your feet. Last night the clouds had unrolled
from the mountains, which were themselves as
visionary as clouds ; the "roof of blue Italian
weather" was here and there decorated by a tapes-
tried vapor, silver or pale gold, gathered up among
the stars and slowly toiling along the calm air.
The sun fell quietly behind the Alps, and the
moment he touched them, it appeared that all the
snows took fire and burned with a candescent brill-
iancy. (I hope you like the opening of my new
novel, as contained in the preceding paragraph.)
Now for Della Scala. It is a vast theatre — six
tiers of boxes, all hung with silk, disposed like our
window curtains, of a light blue or yellow color, the
pit, I should think, almost twice as large as Covent
Garden's. The opera was "Tancredi." Madame
Sesta, the prima donna, old, but generally preferred
to Pasta ; the primo basso, a most extraordinary
singer, with tones more like those of an organ than
any human creature. The scenery is not, in my
opinion, equal to the best at our theatres. One of
the drops was a sort of Flemish painting ; the subject, a village carnival, very well executed. Such
a thing would be novel at C. G. if it could be well,
but it must be very well, done. Now that silk is
so cheap, too, I think they might be a little more

lavish of draperies ; but we are not managers yet.
The ballet, *i baccanali aboliti*, incalculably superior
to ours or the French in the exquisite grace of the
grouping; the countless abundance of dancers, and
the splendor and truth of costume and decoration.
The house was about one-third full, and the people
all talking ; so that there was a buzz — outbuzzing
the Royal Exchange — all the night except during
"Di tanti palpiti." And what else have I seen ?
A beautiful and far-famed insect — do not mistake,
I mean neither the Emperor, nor the King of Sar-
dinia, but a much finer specimen of creation — the
firefly. Their bright light is evanescent, and alter-
nates with the darkness, as if the swift wheeling of
the earth struck fire out of the black atmosphere ;
as if the winds were being set upon this planetary
grindstone, and gave out such momentary sparks
from their edges. Their silence is more striking
than their flashes, for sudden phenomena are almost
invariably attended with some noise, but these
little jewels dart along the dark as softly as butter-
flies. For their light, it is not nearly so beautiful
and poetical as our still companion of the dew —
the glow-worm with his drop of moonlight. If
you see or write to Kelsall, remember me to him ;
and excuse my neglect in not writing to him before

I left England by the plea of hurry, which is true.
To-night at twelve I leave Milan, and shall be at
Florence on Saturday long before this letter tastes
the atmosphere (*pardonnez*, I mean the smoke) of
London.

There and here,

Yours truly,

T. L. BEDDOES.

If you see Mrs. Shelley, ask her to remember
me, and tell her that I am as anxious to change
countries with her as she can be. If I could be of
any use in bringing the portrait, etc., it would be
a proud task, but most likely I only flash over
Florence ; entering on the flood of the stars, and
departing with their ebb.

From C. LAMB.

Enfield, Monday.

DEAR P——, I have more than £30 in my
house, and am independent of quarter-day, not
having received my pension.

Pray settle, I beg of you, the matter with Mr.
Taylor. I know nothing of bills, but most gladly
will I forward to you that sum for him, for Mary

is very anxious that M—— may not get into any
litigation. The money is literally rotting in my
desk for want of use. I should not interfere with
M——, tell M—— when you see him, but Mary
is really uneasy; so lay it to that account, not
mine.

Yours ever and two evers,

C. L.

Do it smack at once, and I will explain to
M—— why I did it. It is simply done to ease her
mind. When you have settled, write, and I'll
send the bank notes to you twice, in halves.

Deduct from it your share in broken bottles,
which, you being capital in your hits, I take to be
two shillings. Do it as you love Mary and me.
Then Elia's himself again.

From GEORGE DARLEY.

MY DEAR PROCTER, — I hardly thank you for
your book; it puts me quite out of conceit with
my own verses. That Hogarthian piece I was
afraid would fail, is most successful; the last
stanza (often so lame) crowns all. I am a
lazzarone of a reader, but have read enough of

your Scrapiana Dramatica to see their merit. Why
not complete a drama? Experience confirms me
more and more in the opinion that a poetic whole ·
is far greater than all its parts unconnected; to
build it up well, forms the true basis of fame. You
must not retail away your stock of dramatic ideas.
It was felicitous ill-luck that the other proofs went
through the devil's hands! I spoil all my own
verses by corrections, and am glad you did'nt
adopt those I had the presumption to offer. One
corrects in such cold blood. The Queen Anne's
men were alone good correctors! As the Rus-
sians rub snow to cure their frozen noses, frigid
writers may be ameliorated by frigid critics.

Any Sunday morn (or other) you like, come
and breakfast; I am always "sociably disposed"
towards you. Drop me a line to expect you, but
don't ask me.

Ever, in all kindliness, yours,

GEORGE DARLEY.

From GEORGE DARLEY.

MY DEAR BARRY CORNWALL, — I am indeed
suspicious, not of you, but myself; most sceptical
about my right to be called "poet," and therefore

it is I desire confirmation of it from others. Why have a score of years not established my title with the world? Why did not "Sylvia," with all its faults, ten years since? It ranked me among the *small* poets. I had as soon be ranked among the piping bullfinches.

Poets are the greatest or most despicable of intellectual creatures. What with ill-health, indolence, diffidence in my powers, and indifference (*now*) to fame, I feel often tempted to go and plant cabbages, instead of sowing laurel seeds that never come up. Verily I court the mob's applause, and care about its censure as much as Coriolanus did; but unless selected judgments are edified, where's the use of writing for the Allseer's perusal and my own?

Glad "Becket" pleases you so far, but dissatisfied (with myself, mind!) that it has only induced you to skim it. For Heaven's sake, unless it *force* you to read it thoroughly, cram it into the blazes! No poetic work that does less is worth a figskin.

Many persons, as well as you, dislike Dwerga; to me it seems, of course, the highest creation in the work. I wrote it with delight, ardor, and ease; how therefore can it well be over-wrought? which would imply artifice and elaboration. I *think* you'll like it better some time hence. T. Carlyle wrote me a characteristic letter; compares "Becket" to Götz von Berlichingen! and predicts vitality. Miss Mitford pronounces me Decker, Marlowe, and Heywood rolled into one! Others too are favorable, but see what *my* great friend the editor of the "Athenæum" has done for me.

A *whole* column of criticism, the censurer cutting the throat of the encomiast all through it! Have I served so long a poetical 'prenticeship to be fubbed off after this fashion?

As to meeting you, fix your own evening; all are alike to me who have no engagements, and cannot be so to you who have many.

About what hour do you generally leave Gray's Inn for St. John's Wood? Let me know that.

Sorry to hear of your annoyances; but what is human life except a chaos of cares?

Ever yours,

GEORGE DARLEY.

Cl. Club. Wednesday.

From G. DARLEY.

Clar. Club, Wednesday, 6 *o'clock.*

DEAR MR. COMMISSIONER, — Confound your prose lunatics who leave you no time for inquirendos upon poetic ones ! Or have you really looked over " Becket," and taken this tender way of telling me you don't like it ?

If you have *not* read it, for God's sake do, and let me know in one word what you think of it. I don't want an essay, or good-natured reserve, neither ; but the single bold word " good " or " bad " — anything except " indifferent."

If my drama cannot prove attractive to selecter judgments, what hope have I from the pig-headed public ?

Never a word more will I write, should " Becket " fail, except for periodicals and mutton-chops.

When you can speak out on the subject, I'll eat and drink with you. Not till then !

Ever yours, poet or not,

THOMAS À-BECKET DARLEY.

From T. CARLYLE.

Chelsea, 25th April, 1844.

DEAR PROCTER, — Thanks for your volume,
and your kind note, both of which are right welcome to me.   I am already far on with the songs:
several of them have been long known to me.
"Our Neighbor's Health," for example, came to
hand through the "Examiner," last winter, and
has stuck, with a curious fascination, ever since.
A just thought, which is itself a bit of harmony,
does deserve and demand to be wedded to its due
tune, its due verse, and to make itself and that
"immortal."   I wish I too had been trained to
sing : it would have been a mighty solacement
to me now and then !

Fulfil your good purposes as to the drama.
The writer of "Mirandola," though he now sniffs
at that composition, cannot be without dramatic
talent.   Nay, a man to whom a thing does look
musical and glorious, will not fail to bring it out
in something of music and glory (that is, of poetry,
as I understand it) through the drama, or *whatever*
way we try it.

There is a Grecian beauty traceable, we are

told, in the shape of the walls of Tiryns, which are built of mere dry boulders, without the aid even of a hammer. What I object to in our damnable dramatists is, that they have in them no *thing*, no event or character, that looks musical and glorious to them — properly no thing at all, but an empty prosing and desire to *have* a thing. How can that escape damnation? Persist, persist? You know what place is paved with good resolutions? The labor is great, but is not the reward also something? Persist, persist!

With many thanks, kind regards, and good wishes in this as in all things,

Yours ever truly,

T. CARLYLE.

From MR. CARLYLE.

5, Cheyne Row, Chelsea.

2nd October, 1843.

DEAR PROCTER, — Many thanks for your kind letter, for your graceful ingenious "Essay on Shakespeare," both of which I have received and read with very great pleasure. The "Essay" abounds in just views, very happily set forth: many of them very far from common among

English critics, or any sort of critics, in this time; to me in letter and spirit they are altogether welcome. Has Themis with her Eldorados stolen you *altogether* from the Muses? I never will believe it.

Rebecca is by no means "beautiful" to look upon: a daughter of Nox, some say of Erebus, too; how can *she* be other than ugly? I was not a little disappointed in Walès generally: a poor, bare, scraggy country, with a poor, bare, scraggy people; the few beautiful objects drowned, generally, in rain and mist; infested on every side by the fatal generation of view hunters! I do not care to look on it again for some time.

You will do me a true kindness if you come down to me here. I sit aloft in my garret, and rarely hear a voice that has much of sphere-melody in it. Do come: in the name of old days, why should you not? If you do not, — not to say if you do, — I myself, on my own resources, will come to Harley Street. My wife joins with me in many kind regards to Mrs. Procter and you. Many blessings and good wishes from

Yours always,
T. CARLYLE.

From LORD JEFFREY.

Penrith.
Thursday Evening, 16*th May,* 1844.

MY DEAR PROCTER, — Your very kind note
of the 12th did not come to my Hertfordshire
home till I had left it, to return to my Scotch
one ; and only came to my hands on my arrival
here this afternoon. I lose no time, therefore,
in now thanking you for all the kind and touching things you have been pleased to put into it
as well as for the book, of which I had read a
short notice in the " Examiner," just before
leaving town, and which brought back so many
pleasing recollections, that I determined to make
myself master of it as soon as I could get it,
and myself, once more into a house of my own.
My friend Empson did not think fit to send it
with the letter ; but I hope to find it waiting
for me at Edinburgh, and promise myself no
little delight, both in renewing my acquaintance with my old favorites, and being introduced by them to the younger members of
the family. If your hand, however, is still as
strong, or even stronger than it was, I cannot

allow the excuse of want of leisure for your letting its improved cunning remain unemployed; and beg to remind you that the more precious the talents are that have been committed to you, the more jealously will an account of the use you have made of them be required. For my part, my hand has waxed feeble, and my little account been made up. My health has long been delicate; and during this last visit to the south, I have had a serious attack of illness, which deprived me (among other gratifications) of the pleasure of seeking out you and Mrs. Procter, and repeating my prayer to you to cheer me with a visit in my Scottish retreat. You will find us, I believe, for the whole remainder of the summer, at a little antique mansion I have about three miles from Edinburgh, called Craig-crook, where you and I may sit up late, and talk about poetry, and youth, and other fantastical things, to the winking stars above, and the rustling weeds around us.

I have a fair remnant of vitality still for such themes and such associates, and can promise that, among the other vices of senility, you shall at least escape the infliction of moroseness or dogmatism.

Do take this into your kind consideration, and

in the meantime believe me always, with great regard,

Your obliged and very faithful

F. JEFFREY.

To B. W. PROCTER, Esq.,

13, *Upper Harley Street.*

From THOMAS HOOD.

Devonshire Lodge,
New Finchley Road,
St. John's Wood.

DEAR PROCTER, — I feel so *sure* that you do not know of my state, or you would come and see me, that I do not hesitate to ask it. I have been three months in bed, and am given over; but, as I have never been quite alive for some years, was quite prepared for such a verdict.

As one of my earliest literary friends, come and say good-bye to

Yours, ever truly,

THOMAS HOOD.

From COUNTESS IDA HAHN-HAHN.

81, *Ebury Street, July 1st,* 1846.

DEAR SIR, — I hope you will be kind enough to understand the meaning of these words. They intend to express my heartfelt thanks for your great kindness in writing for and unto me, and my warm and true admiration of a soul in which high intellects and deep charity are so blended together. If I did understand your English as well as I understand my own German, what a pleasure to write to you! Now, I feel quite as a schoolboy spelling A B C; and yet I must venture to say that I don't agree with you in the idea that " knowledge will civilize us all." The only and only true civilization in which I believe is charity! and charity, my dear sir, springs not from the development of intellects, which we call knowledge, but from the heart; and the hearts are in wilderness whilst the intellects are splendid gardens.

The political economy of the cleverest men in Europe will not change the situation of poor people. They want not skill, but they want love and charity. The world has been created and saved by love and charity. That is the way in which it must be saved a second time. I beg your pardon, dear sir! I know what I *think*, but not quite what I *write*. But believe me to be

Yours most respectfully,
IDA HAHN-HAHN.

Concord, Mass., 30th *September*, 1847.

MY DEAR SIR, — I am not a little gratified by the very kind expressions of your note, and by the little book, which I received a few days since from the hands of Mr. Fields. In the expectation of being in London a little while in the course of the coming winter, the timidities of a home-keeping countryman are in no small degree allayed by the assurance that he has more and better friends in England than he dared to believe.

The valued book you send me is not quite a stranger, though I had-not possessed it before. I find in it some new and some very old acquaintances. One piece of yours, which I knew by heart, I believe five and twenty years ago, " The Pauper's Funeral," I do not find here. I have been enlarging my knowledge of some of your living poets lately; and now again in these pages it occurred as the felicity of England and of every one of her writers, the quiet pride with which she accepts from so many accomplished men the costly gifts of poetic power and culture as only their reasonable service.

In my judgment it is far happier to be one in a chorus of poets, than to wear the bays alone.

> Your obedient servant,
>> R. W. EMERSON.

From H. W. LONGFELLOW.
> *Cambridge, Nov. 28th*, 1847.

MY DEAR SIR, — I thank you very cordially for your friendly note, and the volume of poems you were so kind as to send me by Mr. Fields. Welcome, indeed, they are to me, as such sympathy and such songs must be to every one. No strangers to my fireside are these songs ; we have long looked upon them as among the best in the language, and perhaps the most truly lyric of anything it has to boast. For me they are more suggestive of music than any modern songs whatever, that the three kingdoms have produced. In this point they are rivalled only by a few songs of the olden time, found in the dramatists or the pages of Dryden. Of this kind of poetry I have a very keen enjoyment, and value very highly this present from your hand.

> And as swallows build
> In these wide, old-fashioned chimneys,
> So thy twittering songs shall nestle
> In my bosom.

By the last steamer I sent you a poem which I
have just published on a theme connected with
this country; I hope you will not reject it on
account of the metre. In fact, I could not write
it *as it is* in any other; it would have changed its
character entirely to have put it into a different
measure. Pray agree with me, if you can, on
this point.

My best thanks to your wife for her kind estimate of " Hyperion." Much as I desire it, I am
not now in the right mood to continue the tale.
I hope she will like " Evangeline " as well.

Very sincerely yours,

HENRY W. LONGFELLOW.

From N. HAWTHORNE.

Concord, Massachusetts,
June 17th, 1852.

MY DEAR SIR, — Your very kind little note has
been constantly in my mind, ever since I received
it — being daily remembered, both on account of
the pleasure which it gave me, and because I
purposed a very prompt reply. But (as you will
perhaps recollect) you spoke of a copy of your
poems, which was to accompany the note; and I

waited the receipt of them, in order to have a rich
and abundant theme for my own letter in expressing my sense of their merits. Now, these poems
have never come to hand. They were too precious
to come so far in safety; perhaps your autograph
was in them, and that and the poetry together
have proved too mighty a temptation for some poor
soul, through whose agency the gift was to be
directed hitherward. If anything could subvert
the integrity of our friend Fields himself, it would
be this; but the same might be said of any other
Yankee, for your laurel is especially sacred in the
estimation of us all. We know you well, and love
and admire you in a measure which those who
have you bodily among them can hardly equal.
An English poet should come hither to enjoy the
best part of his fame; at home, he cannot taste
the most refined delight of it, till he be dead,
when, I fear, he will not greatly care to hear about
it, with so many other matters to interest him.

After once flattering myself with the idea of
possessing this volume, from your own hand, I
cannot easily reconcile myself to the loss. If you
would have the great kindness to send another, it
would be most gratefully received. In humble
acknowledgment (but by no means in requital) I

mean to ask your acceptance of a copy of my new romance, which I have written since the receipt of your note, and with many pleasant thoughts that it might have Barry Cornwall for one of its readers.

Very truly, your obliged,
NATHANIEL HAWTHORNE.

From HENRY W. LONGFELLOW.

Cambridge, November 29th, 1852.

MY DEAR SIR, — Mr. Fields brought me safely your friendly salutations and precious volume of songs; but he damped a little the pleasure they gave me, by saying that you had never received a letter I wrote you, some two years ago, acknowledging the receipt of a copy of the edition of 1846. I am really grieved to think that I have been so long associated in your mind with neglect of kindness done me; and that the expression of the wish to hear you and your poetry should have been lost in empty air between us.

The new edition gives me the chance of saying again how much delight your delicious songs have given me, and always are giving me. They are almost the only real *songs* in the language; that

is, lyrics that have the pulsation of music in them.
The Germans and the Spaniards have so many,
and we so few, particularly of late.

Accept also my best thanks for the two volumes
of " Essays and Tales," which I have just received
from Ticknor and Co.   I have not had yet time to
read any of the papers, but the titles are attractive,
and I am sure of great pleasure in them, as I
always get it from your pages.

How much I regret that I did not see you in
London, for who knows when I may be there
again !

Mr. Thackeray is doing very well with his lectures in New York.

With great regard, truly yours,
HENRY W. LONGFELLOW.

From HENRY W. LONGFELLOW.

" We opened twenty-seven papers yesterday,
which contained Barry Cornwall's request, ' Touch
us gently, Time!'   If the old fellow sees this, we
beg him not to meddle with us at all."

Cambridge, June 15*th*, 1853.

MY DEAR SIR,—I write you to-day for two
reasons.   One, because our friend Fields tells me

you " think you owe me a letter." This will make it sure. The second, for the sake of sending you the above paragraph, which I have just cut from a newspaper, and which, if not secured thus to-day, to-morrow will be lost.

On the 1st of June, then (the newspaper is of the 2nd), your beautiful poem — one I am extremely fond of — was in twenty-seven newspapers at least. Now, allowing each say five thousand subscribers, or thereabout, it was on that day left at one hundred and thirty or forty thousand doors; and allowing three or four readers to each paper, read by some half million readers!

Pleasant statistics! . . . And then, in how many other papers has it been, not mentioned by this editor! The best of all is, that it deserves it, and ought to go round through all the papers, once or twice a year, as no doubt it does.

The " old fellow " mentioned in the second sentence is of course Kronos, not Cornwall! The pleasure I have had in seeing this poem so reflected and flashing from thousands of mirrors, makes me hope it will give you pleasure to see it.

Very truly yours,
HENRY W. LONGFELLOW.

From LEIGH HUNT.

Thanks for your thanks, my dear Procter — things which always seem to me so much to call for them, that I suppose it is out of the pure inability of seeing an end to the replication, that no such acknowledgments are made.   You talk of my being ground young again in my writings ; but you ask about the " Mill " in so lively a style of your own, that you seem to be in no want of it.

I rejoice extremely at having pleased you with the inscription, it was your due ; and the nature of the book, I thought, gave me a most apt occasion for saying as much.

Your considerate abstract question, whether boiled chicken with macaroni is not better than mutton, I shall do my best to answer in the concrete next Tuesday, with all the masticatory faculties that are left me.   Monday, I wish I could have said ; — and I thought all days were at my disposal when I wrote last, but a correspondence has since grown upon me, which I do not think I can finish before Monday evening, and I am anxious when I come to you to be able to enjoy my visit without any drawback.

Mrs. Procter has settled my diet capitally well

for Tuesday. *Au reste* it is still the same as what
you so poetically designate, though it shall go hard
if I do not take a glass of claret with you. I
prefer port, but my head differs with me on the
subject; so as I do not like to be left out of more
tabularities than I can help, when I can join them
at all, I take a little of the weakest wine that I can
find which tastes to me the least acid, for otherwise
claret, which has so fine and choice a sound, is
really quite wasted upon me. I perceive nothing
of its famous bouquet; and wine and water would
do quite as well, if it did not oppress me.

As to " old times," great indeed will be my
pleasure in talking about them.

With ever kindest regards,

LEIGH HUNT.

Hammersmith, August 3rd.

One word, please, to make me certain that this
letter has arrived, on account of Tuesday.

From WALTER SAVAGE LANDOR.

Warwick, June 2nd.

MY DEAR SIR,— Immediately on my arrival at
this place I answer your very kind letter, and offer

you my best thanks for your valuable present. Forster can tell you that I expressed to him my regret that I never had had the good fortune to meet you in London. It is only a part of my fault, for I omitted to see, when I might have seen, many old friends. But, in truth, all the time I am in London I am in a fever. I do not know where to go, or what to do.

My friend Ablett will be here within a fortnight. It was he who ordered the printing of that little volume, which, out of pure kindness, you wish to possess. My things in it are really of no value. Indeed, with the exception of my " Agamemnon " and my " Orestes," my poetry in no part satisfies me. Such as it is, it is quite at your service. This I can answer for ; and I will ask Ablett for a copy, the first time I see him.

Your poems have already given me great pleasure, and I know that I have greater in store. Accept my poor thanks for them, and believe me

Your ever obliged

W. S. LANDOR.

From W. S. LANDOR.

Bath, October 2nd.

MY DEAR SIR, — Do not you think I have nearly as much reason to be vexed at your coming to Bath without noticing me, as I have to thank you for your present?

I have been reading it until now, long after bed-time. Only such men as you ought to write about Shakespeare. How dare you talk so boldly of the gentlemen who are come again so highly into favor? · I mean the dramatists who rejoice in the title of Elizabethans, as if that paltry, snarling old bitch ought to give her name to anything so great as even a moderate-sized poet. But all things are now Elizabethan, from poets that nobody can read, to windows that nobody can look out of. They are quite the fashion now, and even our best critics must wear their coats and cravats as ladies and gentlemen say they should. . . . There are few minds so graceful, few contemporaries .so just, as to prefer the " Cenci " and " Prometheus " of Shelley to these bloody bawdries.

What a poet would poor Keats have been, if he had lived! He had something of Shakespeare in him, and (what nobody else ever had) much, very much of Chaucer.

You are a busy man, which is very bad : I am afraid you will be a rich one ; worse and worse.

So you are a Commissioner of Lunacy. I must put on my best behavior when you visit me ; and I request you not to bring forward this letter in evidence against me. But believe me

Your very obliged

WALTER S. LANDOR.

From OLIVER WENDELL HOLMES.

Boston, April 7th, 1858.

MY DEAR SIR, — Mr. Fields has kindly sent me, at your request, a volume of your English songs. Since I first read verses of yours in Hazlitt's " British Poets," your name has always been familiar to me as one of the classics of your century. I have learned your features, too, as well as your songs, for Mr. Fields' author-compelling Zeus of our northern metropolis has one hanging in a place of honor among the votive tablets which adorn his temple.

I need not praise what the world has so long admired. It delights me to know that the world has kept its beauty for you, as it should for every poet, where inspiration is not a mere impulse borrowed from adolescence and vanishing with it.

This little volume will always add sweetness to the beautiful songs it holds, by reminding me that their author has honored me with his kindness.

So soon as I have anything which I am not ashamed to send you, — and I think that may be within a year or two, — I shall do myself the honor of making what poor return I may for your very welcome gift.

With great respect and esteem,

I am yours very truly,

OLIVER WENDELL HOLMES.

Cambridge: Press of John Wilson & Son.

www.ingramcontent.com/pod-product-compliance
Lightning Source LLC
Chambersburg PA
CBHW020953030726
47496CB00005B/1487